BETTER LATE THAN FOREVER

by Shelley Tan

Better Late Than Forever

Never Say Forever, Volume 1

Shelley Tan

Published by Shelley Tan, 2021.

BETTER LATE THAN FOREVER

First edition. August 15, 2021.

Copyright © 2021 Shelley Tan.

ISBN: 979-8215012741

Written by Shelley Tan.

This book is dedicated to my baby.

Dedication:

This book is dedicated to my baby.

Chapter 1- Foreword:

The Happiest Place on Earth

The setting of this book is about the happiest place on earth. However, it is not a book about Disneyland. If you want to know about Disneyland, you should probably just go. Or better yet, go read a brochure, and save your money. Not that I have anything against Disneyland, mind you. Everyone must see it and experience it at least once in their lifetime. And if you are a parent, it is non-negotiable. You must take your child or risk living your life having to tell people for the rest of your life that you were one of *those parents* who never took their child to Disneyland. And then there is the therapy you would have to pay for...but to be clear if you were buying this book because you thought you were going to learn about Disneyland, you were wrong.

Chapter 2 - Sofia

The sun felt beyond incredible as it caressed her backside. Not too hot, not too cold. It was just one of those "made to order" days that couldn't have felt more perfect. There was a cool breeze that melded perfectly with the sun as she lay there in the sand, listening to the soft melody of the water lapping against the shore. The seagulls in the background were far away but still audible, ubiquitous to any beachside town. They cooed and cawed and they scoured the busy streets, barely stopping to notice passersby walking along the sidewalk that circled the small little town. Balboa Island, as it was known, was neither a beachside town nor a resort, it was a little-known island on the coast of Orange County, near the happiest place on earth: Disneyland. Although for Sofia, Disneyland had never been the happiest place on earth. How could it be? Screaming, tired, and spoiled children, long lines, and practically a down payment on a house, just to get in through the

"magic" gates. No, she held fast to a private secret that she was more than content to keep to herself. She knew without a doubt that the happiest place on earth truly was Balboa Island. As she continued to lay on the soft sand and enjoy the warmth from the mid-afternoon sun and the warm salty breeze that washed over her, her mind wandered to her love of the sunshine from the time she had been a chubby little girl, complete with two dark blond, albeit scrawny, pigtails on either side of her head, wrapped up with a bow of yellow yarn. In fact, the brilliance of the sunshine, the smell of freshly cut grass, and the way the early morning dew would sparkle on the flowers in her yard had been so beautiful to her as a young girl that the feeling of it would overwhelm her almost to the point of happy tears. Secretly, she had always wanted her name to be "Sunny," but one of the little girls from school who had the beautiful thick long hair that hung in a single ponytail down her back had been fortunate enough to be named that. Still, she liked her name enough. And as much as she delighted in the young childhood memories of the fresh smell of the grass, the hum of the lawnmower on a Saturday morning, and the brilliance of the water droplets on that lawn or garden, what she most loved was the sun.

Now that she was older, and approaching 50 (was she really that old already?), she still revered, no, worshiped, the sun. Although she worshiped the sun, it was with a healthy dose of respect. At 49 she had definitely matured and didn't underestimate the vast power of the sun as she once had as a teenager when she and her friends used to put oil on and lay by the pool with nothing but their swimsuits on. That had been a costly mistake that took more than a few sunburns to learn. Although she liked to think that she had become not only older but wiser as the years progressed, one thing had never changed, which was her love and respect for the sun. And although she wasn't particularly religious and did not go to church regularly, the sun really was for her, like a god. She often thought of it as the *Giver of Life,* for without it nothing would grow, nothing would live, and the world as we know it would cease to exist. Not only did the sun provide physically, but the sun also fed the soul, produced endorphins from its vitamin D that made people feel good, and so it served as a god in that it fed people spiritually, emotionally, and physically. For some poor individuals, their reliance on the sun had such an effect that they would be diagnosed with seasonal affective disorder during the winter months when there was no sun. This was just one more reason why Balboa Island, located in sunny southern California, was for Sofia and countless others, the best place to be, especially during the winter. It was only natural then, that when she finally made the decision at forty-eight to get her first tattoo, there was no question of what it would be. A beautiful red, orange, and yellow sun, on the inside of her inner right ankle just above the bone, was the perfect symbol. Putting it on her ankle meant that she would always have the sun with her, day in, day out, forever...

And so it was that perhaps more than ever she needed the reassurance that something would last forever, for everything that year had seemed to turn dark. The world was going through the Covid pandemic, the country had never been more divided, and to top it all off, her marriage of 17 years had just come to an end. The sun on her ankle was a symbol of better times, of happiness past and yet to come. It was hope that she could carry around on her ankle that would always be there, no matter what. This is why she decided the time had come—she packed up her bags, put her house up for rent, and quit her job. As she lay now on the beach outside Opal Avenue on

Balboa Island, she couldn't have been more content. She continued to lay there in total bliss, thinking that the next time she came outside to lay by the bay she would have to bring at least a glass of white wine, probably a chenin blanc or pinot grigio, as that was the only thing she could think of to top off the moment. Unfortunately, her reverie was short-lived, as she felt the nagging but urgent need to pee. "Damn it!" she screamed inside her head. Although she had never had a large bladder, this was another physical sign that she was, in fact, aging. In fact, she had earned the dubious distinction of being called "the pee queen" in high school, as she took every liberty to use the ladies' room in between passing periods just to be able to make it through the class. Almost 30 years and two babies (twins, in fact) later, the situation had definitely not improved. And with that, she stood up, shoved her feet through her pink flip-flops, grabbed her striped beach towel, and quickly walked back to the cottage she was renting on Opal Avenue.

Once back at her rental and after a quick trip to the bathroom, Sofia succumbed to her next urgent bodily need, her stomach, which was aching with hunger. Although she had always been a healthy eater, she had always had a huge appetite for as long as she could remember. She used to hear stories when she was little about how she should "suck in your stomach" (she was), "watch it when you get older" (she did), and how "If I ate as much as you, I would weigh 300 pounds!" (Thank God, she didn't!) Although she had always been slim, at five feet seven inches tall and 49 years old, she now weighed 150 pounds, putting her as the definite heavyweight amongst the women in her immediate family. She reached into the fridge and took out the usual: ingredients for a salad, knowing full well she would be hungry exactly three hours later, right before bed, and probably end up eating again. *Oh well,* she thought to herself, *I have to at least try, especially now that I am on Balboa Island, the Happiest Place on Earth, where everyone is skinny, rich, and seemingly perfect...*

It was true, in fact, that one of the things that made Balboa so great was also the same thing that put extra pressure on Sofia: the fact that everyone seemed to have a money tree in their back or front patio (although she reckoned it must be in the back patio, out of sight, because as much as she tried she had never seen one), and the fact that everyone there was blonde, and skinny. The blonde part she could handle with a quick monthly trip to her hairdresser Marci, but as for the skinny part? Most on the island were a size 0 or 2. She was definitely closer to a size 10 or 12. And no, she was not so desperate to fit in that she was willing to go under the knife. She had heard far too many horror stories, and seen firsthand how the weight came back on, and then some, years later.

Besides, she had much more important things to spend her money on, and furthermore, she valued her health way too much and wasn't going to risk it. No, she would have to do things the old-fashioned way, meaning she would have to watch what she ate and work out more. She decided that after she got more settled she would think about getting a trainer. Perhaps one that wasn't too cost-prohibitive. Perhaps she could give her friend Char a call. Char said she had a good friend, Valerie Parker, who had also just recently gotten out of a divorce and was just getting started as a personal trainer. Yes, she nodded to herself, that's what I will do. Enough was enough. She certainly wasn't getting any thinner standing around thinking about it. She decided then and there, that she would definitely hire a trainer, and call her friend immediately, just as soon as she landed a job.

Chapter 3 - Duke

Duke woke up around 9 a.m. wearing his usual gray boxer shorts and nothing else. Like many nights, he had fallen asleep drinking beer and watching TV the night before, on the couch, with all of the windows open. Even the front door was left ajar, for the cat, Bonkers, to be able to come and go as he pleased. *Why have a litter box,* rationalized Duke, *when there is a whole beach full of sand just yards from the house?* Although he wasn't on a budget, Duke definitely didn't want to "waste" the money buying cat litter when he didn't need to. Furthermore, as a bachelor, housekeeping wasn't his first priority, and not having to contend with a litter box was one less chore he had to deal with each week. Duke poured himself a cold cup of leftover coffee that was still in the pot from the day before and quickly nuked it for 30 seconds before stepping outside barefoot to drink it. *Now, where is that damn cat?* He didn't give it another thought before sitting down to see if there were any girls outside already tanning themselves in bikinis. Perhaps he could get lucky and spot a few girls already sunning themselves as he drank his coffee. One of his favorite features of his Balboa beach house on Opal Avenue was the front patio with a direct view of the marina, bay, and scantily clad women. He was out of luck, as the only thing on the beach beside the seagulls were the beach towels. It was common for the residents of Balboa to go out early, leave a beach towel in order to "stake their claim" and come out later when the weather had warmed up to sunbathe. Just as he was going back inside, he heard a noise from next door. At the same time, he unknowingly brought in more than a few grains of sand that were stuck to the bottom of his feet along with him. He thought the noise next door must be his new neighbor and hoped that she would be good-looking, and single. Well, good-looking was a must, he thought, while being single was optional, but preferred, as he liked to keep things simple. As he strolled through his TV room and made his way to the kitchen, he caught a glimpse of himself in the mirror, which was hanging on the wall in front of a dent that had occurred one evening that he doesn't entirely remember. Apparently, it had been enough fun that his neighbor had complained. As he caught a glimpse of his six-foot-two-inch frame, he could see the rippled muscles in his arms bulging beneath his tanned skin. His disheveled hair, mostly brown with a few strands of sun-kissed blonde from his time spent surfing off the Balboa Pier, and his own natural brown, hung below his ears in wavy sections that all the girls seemed to find sexy. Other than the massive amount of hair on his head, the rest of his body was relatively smooth, devoid of any chest, back, or facial hair. Besides the brown (rather than surfer blonde) hair, he looked like a typical southern California beach bum. His phone rang, derailing his thoughts of his appearance to more pressing matters: work. Rather than answer the phone, he decided to let it go to voicemail, and instead hopped in a cool and quick shower, threw on a buttoned short sleeve shirt with some khaki cargo shorts, and ran outside to hop in his Jeep. The fresh ocean air on the way to work would dry his thick hair, and brushing his teeth would have to wait. Instead, he reached for a tin of cinnamon Altoids and popped two in his mouth.

Chapter 4 - Char

It was 5 a.m. and Char's alarm clock was blaring. If she turned it off and skipped her workout with Val, she would be able to gain another hour and a half of sleep. Instead, she thought about what else she would gain, mainly a bunch more weight in her thighs and butt, and decided to roll out of bed instead. Although Char had been a cheerleader in high school at Newport Harbor High School, it was getting harder and harder to keep her figure as the years had passed and she had other priorities besides working out all day. Recently her longtime friend, Valerie, had been forced to close her catering job as the Covid pandemic hit, and was looking to reinvent herself.

"Why don't you become a personal trainer?" Char had suggested. "You are always working out and you already know how to run a business." Besides, Char offered, "I've put on five pounds recently and I'm having trouble taking it off. I'll be your first client and I can help you spread the word. With this beautiful weather, we could work out on the beach, and we can social distance while we have our sessions!" Valerie really didn't know what to say, but considering she was living on credit cards and had no other prospects for income, decided to take her sweet friend up on her offer. "All right," Valerie agreed, "but I won't charge you until you start losing weight!" Valerie knew her friend would never let her go unpaid, especially given her current financial situation, but she had to suggest it so as to not appear to take Char for granted. Now the time had come, and Char was forced to put her money where her mouth had been...literally. *How bad can it be?* Char asked herself. *It's not like I don't do ANY exercise to stay in shape...*

As was typical on Balboa Island, Char enjoyed getting up and "working out" each day with a brisk walk along the border of the island, exactly three miles from her house, to the ferry which takes you across the harbor to Newport, and back. She enjoyed participating in this ritual that the majority of weight-conscious women partook in; it made her feel as though she too, was a classic "Balboan", or was it "Balbonian"? Either way, it was good exercise, not too exerting, and allowed for the occasional Balboa Bar without tipping the scales; that is, until recently. Now she was going to have to step it up. As she rolled out of bed and put on her black Nikes and yoga pants, she muttered "Just do it," and realized she had probably seen one too many Nike commercials.

Chapter 5 - Katrina

Tuesday, Tuesday, Tuesday... thought Katrina woefully, as she reviewed the long list of required meetings that lay before her that day. First, she had to attend a leadership meeting with all of the directors of the varying departments, then she had to interview for a new principal, followed by a meeting with an unhappy parent...all before lunch. Although she had enjoyed her quick rise through the ranks in education and resulting salary increases, she definitely earned every penny, she thought. At 55 years old, Katrina, "Kat" as she was known, was definitely thinking about life beyond being a school superintendent. The stress of her job had taken its toll, and with no one other than her cats to keep her company, Kat, who was starting to feel every bit her age (and some days beyond), enjoyed coming home to her luxury condo, also on Balboa. At that moment her secretary, Molly, knocked on her office door to let her know that her 12 o'clock interview was here. "An hour early? I still have leadership!" Kat replied. Then, thinking twice, changed her mind about leadership for today as she could do with one less meeting. "All right, send her in. What's her name again?"

"Sofia, ma'am. Sofia Carter. Shall I give you a few minutes?"

"Yes...then send her back. Let's get this interview underway. I need a new principal for Harbor Street Elementary." Kat gave herself a quick once over. She was wearing her favorite pair of Cole Haan shoes, slip-on flats that were both classic and comfortable. At this stage of her career, despite being in southern California, she decided that if she had to decide between being fashionable or comfortable, she would be comfortable. With her Cole Haans, she believed she had effortlessly achieved both. The rest of her outfit was conservative yet professional, as her broad shoulders fit snugly into her navy blazer and matching slacks. Her dark hair was cut short, and her favorite feature about herself was her blue-green eyes that changed color depending on her outfit.

She wore no jewelry or makeup, as it just never felt like "her."

Chapter 6 - Sofia

Sofia sat anxiously in the entryway of the Newport-Mesa superintendent's office, reading her notes about Harbor Street Elementary, as she really needed a job. When her marriage had ended, with all that seemed to be wrong in the world, she had needed a change. She quit her principal job in northern California to return to her roots, to her happy place...to the sunshine. *I need this*, she thought. *I deserve this,* she told herself. She felt mildly guilty about leaving Kevin and Matthew behind back home, but they *were* 18, in college, and didn't want to uproot their lives to come with her. Besides, they had girlfriends, and at 18, Sofia conceded, that was far more important to them than following their mom. So here she was, at 49, starting over. She took a deep breath to calm her nerves, thought about the money she had in her savings account, and...

"Sofia," Sofia looked up and saw Molly standing in front of her, with a clipboard, smiling.

"If you are ready, I can show you in. Ms. Anderson will see you now."

In an effort to sound more confident than she felt, Sofia took another deep breath, stood up, and with an equally big smile, beamed "Yes, thank you." It had been a long time since she had had to look for a job, and her small school in northern California felt like small potatoes compared to this. *You have the experience, you got this*, she told herself.

Her first impression of Ms. Anderson was not what she expected, nor was it particularly striking. Sofia realized she expected Ms. Anderson to look more, well, like a well-dressed version of the ladies she saw walking on Balboa Island: sporty, blonde, young. Ms. Anderson was a refreshing variant of this norm. It was nice not to have *EVERYONE* in southern California look like a Barbie, she thought. In her own insecure way, she realized, this somehow made her feel better about herself.

Well, thought Sofia, as she was walking to her car after the meeting, *fingers crossed*. As she drove her Mazda sedan back over the highway and onto the bridge with the beautiful colored flags that flanked both sides, she felt physically relaxed. As she looked at the rainbow of colors on the varying flags in purple, blue, green, yellow, orange, and red, she chuckled to herself. *Was the irony lost on everyone but me? Or do I just have a twisted mind?* Where she lived in northern California, close to San Francisco, a rainbow was the symbol used to support the LGBTQ movement. *Ha! Definitely not meant to symbolize that down here, not in conservative Orange County,* she thought.

While Sofia considered herself to be "straight", she had a sister who had been with both men and women. There were times during the course of her marriage that she respected, almost admired, her sister's relationship with her partner and lamented the fact that she just wasn't attracted to women. The women that her sister had been with, at least, just seemed to be more considerate than typical male counterparts, and more sensitive than her husband had been. Everyone seemed to agree that in general, women mature faster than men. At 49 she was still waiting for her ex-husband to grow up...

Speaking of men, as she pulled up to her condo on Opal she saw her neighbor, Mr.

Gorgeous, outside wearing his usual...shorts? Boxers? Swim trunks? She really couldn't tell and didn't care. She thought how fortunate she was to have two nice views to look at each day out her window: the harbor, as well as the neighbor, Mr. What's His Name. He looked to be about 20 years younger than her, perhaps 25. *Oh well,* she thought. It was too early for her to start a relationship anyway when she was getting settled and all. You know what they say about

"rebound" relationships... Besides, it would be better just to have him as a friend, you know, someone to help her out around the house, if needed. She wasn't exactly a natural in the maintenance department, having never been on her own.

As she stepped out of her car, she caught his eye. "Hi! I'm Sofia! Nice to meet you!" She smiled her flashiest smile; a little innocent flirtation wouldn't hurt, right?

She felt her heart palpitate, or was that a skipped beat? As he swung around his gorgeous, wavy, sun-stroked hair flipped back behind his ears, he looked her way. She could practically smell the sea salt on him from her driveway next door...mmmmm.

"What's up? I'm Duke. You must be my new neighbor?"

Duke? Really, his name is Duke? she thought to herself. *Seriously?* Of course, it is...this is southern California, she reminded herself. Of course, his name is "Duke". When she was growing up in unpretentious northern California, she had a neighbor whose German shepherd was named Duke. But this was southern California. *So okay, it's "southern California edgy"...I suppose.*

"Nice tattoo," he said as he nodded at her ankle. Inwardly, she was doing a triple flip but managed to play it cool with an equivalent nod in return.

"Thanks," she said. "See ya around." And with that, she went inside to grab her swimsuit, and a glass of chardonnay, as she was out of her sauvignon blanc that she had so desired the last time she went to lie on the beach.

Chapter 7 - Char

To the rest of the beachgoers at Newport Beach, Char may have appeared dead. If she didn't appear dead, she thought, she at least felt it. She hadn't worked out that hard since, well, since forever, and could barely breathe, let alone move. Did Valerie have some pent-up aggression against her? Or was she really just doing the job that Char had hired her to do? *Holy crap!* she thought as she lay there still, as dead as a starfish, and spread out face down in a similar fashion as she imagined a dead starfish would look. Valerie must really need the cash since she promised to bill her only when she started losing weight. *Well, considering I am stuck here, face down, on the beach with no foreseeable prospect of moving ever again, I may just starve to death right here. When the tide comes in, perhaps it can just sweep me quietly out to sea...Okay, drama queen,* she thought. *Quit being so maudlin, you are not going to die!*

Char had plenty to do, which is why she planned her workout for the first thing in the morning, but now she was wondering what, if anything, would be accomplished the rest of today. As much as she loved Valerie (they were practically sisters), perhaps she could have offered to help her friend out with her cash flow problem in a different way. It may have been better to just have given her the cash, considered it a loan, than this torture. *And I'm paying for this? I must be going crazy,* she considered. *Who in their right mind pays to be tortured?*

Char knew she was lucky, even if she didn't feel it at this particular moment. She had moved from a run-down apartment in Costa Mesa to Balboa Island five years ago, after receiving a rather large sum of money after her mother's death. While her own mother had had some financial ups and downs as a horse trainer in Santa Barbara, she had property bequeathed to her from her grandmother that was passed on to Char at the time of her mother's death. In California, a few acres in Santa Barbara yielded quite a hefty sum, enough for Char to get a small place on Balboa with a manageable monthly mortgage. However, if she didn't get off this beach soon and drag herself into work, she may not have the money for that mortgage...

After finally making it home, into the shower, and pouring herself an iced coffee, Char mustered up enough energy to at least feel grateful to Val, even if she physically still felt like the dead starfish she envisioned lying on the beach. Valerie, who was ten years older than Char, looked absolutely amazing. Everything about her exuded health, down to the tips of her eyelashes! Yes, even her eyelashes were super long, thick, and dark. *I guess this is the effect when one takes care of themselves,* she thought. Valerie was not only uber-healthy with her diet—easy to understand, so hard to do...fruits, vegetables, whole grains, lean protein. No chips, saturated fat, sugar...or fun. Until her divorce, she never even indulged in a glass of wine! On the other hand, the reward was that she looked 35 rather than 58, had the body of a Barbie, had no body fat, gorgeous skin, hair, nails...down to her eyelashes. She exuded health. Valerie not only talked the talk, but she was also the gal who walked the walk. It was not a fad, diet, or anything else for Val, other than a lifestyle that she had been following forever. And now, she was going to make a living out of her passion. *If I could have just a little of this rub off on me,* thought Char, as she debated rewarding herself for her workout with the last of the chips and salsa and a margarita to wash it down, *I would be so far ahead of the game!* She instead decided to swap the margarita for a glass of wine, and well, that was better than having the margarita, so she decided she deserved the chips and salsa. As she sipped on her wine and enjoyed her chips, she tried to mentally prepare for tomorrow's workout. Val worked out six days a week, and Char was going to have to do the same. Gulp!

Chapter 8 - Duke

The contrast between Duke's liberal attitude and the conservative county in which he lived in was vast. And although his liberal views were controversial, this controversy also made for interesting talk radio, and Duke's "Dusk to Dawn" segment on KXQX drove up the ratings. Yes, many conservatives were pissed off and angry when he discussed topics that supported LGBTQ rights, a woman's right to choose, or more restrictions for gun owners, but increased ratings meant increased revenue, and at the end of the day, it was the ratings that made the station money. So while Duke got to sleep in, surf, head to the beach, and otherwise enjoy the trappings that Orange County had to offer, he also had a chill job that allowed him to do what he did best: talk. And okay, he kind of enjoyed pissing people off, so that part of the job was actually fun for him. In fact, he tried to model himself off of Howard Stern, someone who he had grown up listening to and thought of as a role model.

As much as he liked his job, this particular year had been difficult, between the Covid pandemic and the state of race relations in the country. Never had Duke seen the nation so divided, or people so angry, or sensitive. It was almost hard to tease or lighten the mood because everyone got so darn offended these days! What happened to the good old days when people knew how to take a joke? And even though Duke lived in and loved Orange County and Balboa Island, he was originally from Berkeley and had brought his liberal attitudes with him. He never anticipated that things would get this bad, that he would really have to watch what he said. This was particularly difficult for him as part of his appeal to his audience was riding that line, being edgy, a bit offensive, and yes, at times, crass.

As he left the station around 2 a.m., he hopped back in his open-air Jeep, not bothering to put the sides or top-up, and wound his way down Highway 101 toward Balboa Island. It was midFebruary, and although it was cool, the air was not chilly like it was up north this time of year. Duke breathed the cool salty-sweet air deep into his lungs, as he felt the moisture that lingered in the air from the Pacific coast caress his skin. Even though it was 2 a.m., it was a full moon, and the reflection of the moon shimmered along the coastline, illuminating the shoreline below. Far in the distance, a few lights were still visible in a few of the houses. Palm trees stood out among the backdrop as they were highlighted by the moon. Duke admired his surroundings as he pulled onto Marine Ave. and crossed the bridge onto the island. He passed by the chic boutiques that were now darkened and quiet. There was so much hustle and bustle outside of the quaint shops and restaurants during the day, that having odd hours was an added benefit to Duke's job, as he could drive straight through to his house without sitting in traffic as people pulled in and out of the various shops and restaurants. As a popular vacation resort, the traffic was particularly nightmarish during the summer months when tourism was at its height. On occasion when Duke got home from work and needed to unwind, he would grab his surfboard, drive around Coast Highway to Newport Pier, and night surf. Tonight was the perfect night for that, as it was easier to see with the full moon, and he thought seriously about grabbing his board once he got home tonight. He would come home around sunrise, right as the early morning surfers were heading out. Instead, he grabbed a beer, turned on the TV, and as usual, fell asleep.

Chapter 9 - Sofia

The phone rang at precisely 10 a.m. and Sofia rushed to answer it, hoping it was one of her twins. Although she had been a principal and had always had to work, her first priority had always been being a mother, and it was difficult for her to be so far away from the two true loves of her life, even though she knew she needed to do this for her. *Perhaps once they come down to visit me,* she thought, *they might consider moving out this way.* What teenage boys wouldn't want to live down here? And certainly, there would be more job opportunities here than where they were currently living...

An unfamiliar voice was at the other end of the phone, "Hello? Yes? Yes, this is her." She quickly changed gears, as it was not Kevin or Matthew on the other end. It was Molly, the secretary from Harbor Street Elementary where she had applied for a principal job last Friday. Her voice and tone immediately perked up to express both professionalism and enthusiasm, in a meager attempt to change secretary Molly's mind in case she was calling to deliver bad news. Not that the secretary had that power anyway, she knew full well, but still, it couldn't hurt...

Sofia couldn't believe her luck! She couldn't remember being this elated in a very long time. She had been offered the position and the life that she reimagined was coming together! She would be the new principal of Harbor Street Elementary in the Newport-Mesa School District! Not only that, she would be able to keep her rental on Balboa for as long as she wanted, which would be forever, barring some unseen unfortunate circumstance. Or, she thought, optimistically, maybe she would stop renting only to buy a nice little fixer-upper. It likely wasn't affordable on a principal's salary, but then again, one never knew...

After she recovered from her initial shock (she had a job!) Sofia took a minute to celebrate. She poured a healthy glass from the open bottle of chardonnay; it was going to go bad soon anyway and why waste it? She took a moment to think of her dad. Every time something good happened, she naturally thought of her dad, as before her twins, he had always been her favorite person, and she loved making him proud. She knew that landing this job (only her second interview!) would make him proud. In fact, it brought back one of her most cherished Balboa Island memories, of when she had been a young girl, vacationing with her family here, when her dad also got "THE CALL."

Having been a successful civil litigator in private practice for many years, her dad had applied, uncontested, for a position as a Superior Court Judgeship in Sacramento at the exact time the family was going on their annual vacation to Balboa. This was before cell phones, and her dad was expecting an important phone call from Governor Deukmejian to confirm his appointment. Her dad was not the type to let down his family and cancel or even postpone the trip, so he simply walked around the island until he found a payphone, which there happened to be right outside the small, local market on the corner of Marine and Park Avenues. It was on that trip that the entire family had stood by excitedly as he got the call...and an annual toast of champagne in commemoration of the historic moment that took place at the phone booth each year thereafter. As Sofia sat back with her glass of wine, a contented smile crossed her face. She was going to call her dad, to tell him that she, too, had a "telephone moment" on Balboa Island. She hoped that she would also be having a commemorative toast in honor of her new position, year after year. She may even walk down to the exact spot of the famous phone booth to have her own celebration.

The phone booth had been removed years ago, as no one used them anymore, but still, it didn't matter. It was the thought that counted and a way to mentally connect with her dad.

Chapter 10 - Valerie

Valerie woke up and fell back to sleep for the umpteenth time. Something just wasn't quite right. Was she coming down with something? She certainly hoped it wasn't the coronavirus that had been going around. She did a quick inventory of how she was feeling and tried to compare that to the known symptoms of the coronavirus—sore throat, no, fever...no, headache, body aches, and sleepy, yes. She didn't have the classic signs, but again, it seemed like everything these days was a sign of Covid. She called Char to cancel her workout with her. Not that she could afford it, but she just couldn't stomach it today. Literally, something in her abdomen hurt and all she wanted to do was sleep. She called Char, but it went to voicemail.

"I am so sorry, Char, that I have to cancel but I think I may be coming down with something," she said. "I'm going to go back to sleep. When I wake up, I will make an appointment to get a Covid test. If you have it in you, I want you to do the workout we did yesterday, which includes the warmup we did, the exercises to get your heart rate up and boost your metabolism. Do four rounds if you are able and rest when you need to. Watch your form...and lay off the booze.

Okay Char, talk soon. Love you, bye!"

Valerie was no sooner off the phone than she rolled over in bed, listening to the waves until she was asleep. This wasn't like her, falling asleep in the middle of the day. She never had been much of a napper. She believed it was a waste of time and for weak people. Valerie prided herself on being strong, and that did not include napping. But today, she just couldn't fight it off as the clock ticked past 2 p.m. It would be five hours later before she woke up. When she did finally wake, she felt rested but was still in pain. She took to the internet to see if the coronavirus could cause abdominal discomfort, and vowed to see her doctor first thing in the morning. It had been an unproductive day and Valerie chastised herself for not making her workout and failing to meet her one and only client.

Chapter 11 - Katrina

It was once again Monday morning and Katrina felt no more rested than she had when she had left on Friday afternoon to go home for the weekend. She liked Balboa Island, but most of her friends lived far away, as she cultivated friendships through her work but had been forced to move as she rose the ranks and took higher ranking positions wherever they had been available. So now she found herself in southern California, Orange County, Balboa Island, to be exact. She enjoyed many aspects of it, the weather, her salary that had increased by at least 20%, and her own place with a view of the ocean. It was peaceful and quiet, and she could walk down to several bars and restaurants after work to get dinner or a drink without having to worry about driving and getting caught up in the horrible southern California traffic that escalated her blood pressure.

In addition to her friends whom she kept in close contact with through extended phone calls after work and during the weekends, Kat had her two orange tabby cats, Jake and Annie, who were her babies. Although she had been married once many years ago, her marriage hadn't lasted because her husband seemed to have interests outside the marriage, interests that made Kat question which team he was on sexually. Why would he leave on her birthday to go camping with the guys if he was in love with Kat? It made no sense. After two years of marriage, Kat called it quits and walked out on him, leaving him with all the bills. Not that she wasn't an honest or fair person, quite the contrary, in fact. But screw him! What sort of man leaves his wife home alone on her birthday to go camping with his male "friends"? No. And furthermore, he had bought the new couch set without even consulting her, so why should she pay? Anyway, life was full for her now without any complications. Besides, she loved her cats tremendously and they didn't betray her as her ex had. At this point in her life, who needs men anyway? Her cats were sweet, loving, cuddly, and besides, they never judged her. She fed them gourmet cat food and bottled water exclusively, and in return, they never judged her for the wine that she consumed. Nope, they loved her unconditionally. And besides, she rationalized, are you really drinking alone if your cats are there with you? Between her friends, her career, her cats, and her wine clubs, she lived a fulfilling life and was very independent. Besides, Orange County was not the place she would find her type anyway. Everyone was so materialistic and focused on superficial traits. She wanted to find someone with some substance, or go solo. As it turned out, she found out years later that her exhusband Paul had in fact finally come out as gay (no huge surprise there), had moved to San Francisco, and had been working at an upscale French restaurant as a chef. Other than the cooking, there was little else that Kat had missed about Paul. However, the irony was not lost on her, as she had taken years of Latin and knew what the Latin name for Paul meant: small.

One of her favorite things each night after she came home from work was to watch her two tabbies, Jake and Annie, walk down the hallway together on their "dinner date," where their gourmet cat food would be waiting for them. Like any mother, telling Jake and Annie apart was easy for her: Jake was shy, had longer fur, and had more white on his coat. Besides that, his feet were huge. By contrast, Annie was very thin, always getting into mischief, and mostly orange. The funny thing about this was that when friends did come to visit, they couldn't tell the difference between Jake and Annie. How was this possible? Just like a mother of twins who thinks her children look nothing alike, Jake and Annie were distinct, not only in personality but in appearance too.

Even though she felt run down and that the weekend had been far too short, Kat went online to do her health assessment as she had done every day since the Covid pandemic had begun: No fever, cough, sore throat, diarrhea, or runny nose. Yep, she was good to stay at work. *Yaaaaay,* she thought sarcastically. She next went online to check her calendar for the day to see just how many meetings she was going to have to attend. At least one major task was off her to-do list: she had hired her new elementary school principal. That would be a load off as the parents were getting antsy and she didn't like having to juggle the school along with her superintendent duties anyhow. As far as the new principal was concerned, Katrina didn't give her much thought, other than she obviously had made a positive impression; otherwise, she wouldn't have hired her. She seemed cute, bubbly, and had an upbeat personality. She also knew some Spanish and had a lot of experience. As Kat took her position seriously, she was happy to have found a principal who had some experience, and who seemed like she would be fun to work with. With that task checked off her list, Kat began to delve into her day, starting with the mass of emails that had piled up overnight. After grabbing a last cup of coffee for the day, she sat down and began to sift through the mass, deleting the irrelevant ones first. By the time she got through the pile, it was time for lunch, and so Kat told Molly she would be back shortly and went to grab some fast food. She couldn't wait until next Monday when Sofia would be starting at the elementary school.

Chapter 12 - Char

What the hell? thought Char after listening to Valerie's message on her phone. *This is so not like her. Valerie really better be sick, because if she blew me off for a date or some cute guy...that would be really messed up.* Char thought about it some more, and then immediately recanted, feeling guilty for having had such a negative and untrue thought about her friend. *Of course, Valerie would never flake on me to go out with some guy. Besides,* she thought, *our workouts are scheduled for 9 a.m. No one has a date at 9 a.m.* She then spent the next 15 minutes berating herself for her terrible thoughts about her good friend before deciding to call her. Char picked up her phone and dialed Val. Nothing. *Hmmm,* she thought. *Now I'm getting worried.* Perhaps she could call their mutual friend, Sofia, and see if she had heard anything. Valerie took her cell phone out of her pocket and called Sofia. It went straight to voicemail. *I wonder if she is at the interview for the principal job that she told me about?*

After waiting for Sofia's phone to go to her voicemail, Char left a message.

"Hey Sofia, it's me, Valerie. Char and I had a workout planned for today, and I haven't heard from her. I'm starting to get worried. I am going to head over to her house and see if she is okay. Call me if you get this message. Bye!"

Char called into work and hopped into her Mercedes convertible. She headed down Highway 1 to Corona del Mar where Valerie lived, alone. When she got there, Gus, her gray pit bull mix, greeted her out front and led her to the door. Char knocked at the door and waited. She knocked again, and again, she waited. Nothing. Finally, Char reached the knob on the front door and gently twisted it, calling to Valerie as she slowly opened it. Still, nothing. At this point Gus was running back and forth between Valerie's room and Char's, trying to communicate to Valerie that she had a visitor. The only problem was that Valerie was sound asleep, and was used to Gus running amok. Besides, she felt so bad that neither an earthquake nor a tsunami would have roused her...

Char wound her way to the back of the house where she found Valerie asleep in her bed, still, in her workout clothes, tennis shoes kicked off by the foot of the bed. Gus ran back to the bed and picked up one of the shoes, imploring Valerie to engage in a game of fetch. "Go, Gus!" she said. "Not now! I need to see if Val is okay..."

"Valerie...Valerie...Valerie...Valerie..." Char must have whispered her name close to 10 times before Valerie finally rolled over and opened one eye, half-mast, and looked at Char. She then grabbed her lower abdomen and writhed in pain, her face in a grimace that Char didn't recognize. Small beads of sweat began to pool on her forehead. Under the stress, or maybe as phantom pain, suddenly Char began to feel hot and sweaty and her stomach was soon in a knot as well.

"Come on, Val..." she beseeched her. "Get up. Let me get you some water. You feel hot.

Did you get your Covid test yet? We need to get you checked out," Char said as she instinctively reached inside her purse for her hand sanitizer and mask. When Char finally walked Valerie to the car in Valerie's driveway, Gus was already waiting inside. "Gus! Get out!" said Char. In her haste and panic, Char must have left the car door open, and Gus, never missing an opportunity, had jumped in. He still had Valerie's left sneaker hanging from his mouth by its shoelace, with drool and slobber all over it. "Alright," Char conceded, "You can come...just hand over the sneaker..." Later, at Hoag Hospital in Newport Beach, Valerie was resting comfortably while Gus and

Char waited in the car. Char's cell phone rang, and she picked it up, noticing it was Sofia returning her call.

"Hey, I got your message. Have you heard from her? Is everything okay?" Char could hear the panic in Sofia's voice.

"Yeah," Char said. "So there's actually been a bit of bad news." "Oh my god! What is it?" Sofia interrupted, panicking.

"Well, I'm not sure yet, exactly," Char admitted. "But I went over to Valerie's house, and she wouldn't wake up. When she finally did, she had terrible abdominal pain. I'm here at Hoag Hospital. She's been admitted."

"Do you think it's Covid?" Sofia asked, without stopping to think, "Oh wait, you said abdominal pain. That's not Covid, is it?" Sofia wondered.

"I don't know anything at the moment, but as soon as I hear anything, I'll give you a call."

"Alright," Sofia said, "Don't forget."

Char promised Sofia that she wouldn't.

No visitors were allowed in the hospital due to the Covid pandemic, so the hospital promised to call Char on her cell phone as soon as they had some information to share. While Char waited, she combed through the headlines on her news app and sighed. What has happened to the country over the last four years? It seemed as though everything she heard on the news was depressing, beyond the norm. Race relations, police shootings, the Covid pandemic...it was all so sad. Just yesterday she was listening to Duke's Dusk to Dawn program on the radio when another report of a police shooting of a black man, who had been unarmed, had occurred. For a nation that had been proud of being a model for the world by celebrating its inclusion and diversity, suddenly that was being called into question as Asian Americans were being targeted due to the "China Virus" (as President Trump liked to refer to it), people were afraid to get on airplanes with someone of Muslim descent, and children were being separated from their parents at the Mexican-American border. It was enough to bring even the most ardent optimist down. And now, just when she was starting to work out and take care of herself, her good friend Valerie was in the emergency room.

"Come on Gus," she said, "what do you want? We're going through the drive-through. Want a hamburger?" Maybe it was her imagination, but it seemed to her that even Gus was looking depressed. "At least we have each other, old boy," she said. With that, she put the key in the ignition and pulled out of the hospital parking lot. They were on a mission for the nearest burger joint.

Chapter 13 - Sofia

Her alarm must have been set wrong because there was no way it could be 6 a.m. already. But when she looked out the window Sofia could see the sunrise coming up in the east and hear the sounds of the early morning garbage pickup and realized that it was already Monday morning and the first day of her new job. Although she usually started each day with a workout, today she decided to skip it, instead using the time to primp until she felt that every hair on her blonde head was just so. She had used the job offer as an opportunity to stop by Neiman Marcus in Fashion Island, as she always felt more confident when she liked how she looked. And if she felt confident, she rationalized, she would be more confident, thus allowing her to make good decisions and excel in her new position. So really, she continued to rationalize, the new outfit was a career investment, just like a student loan for graduate school might be. She had picked out the most beautiful plumcolored skirt and matching blazer. The skirt fell just to her knee and the blazer fit her beautifully. She had cream-colored nylons and a soft silk cream-colored blouse under her blazer. Her lack of an appropriate shoe to complete her look was what had led her next to Nordstrom, yet another investment in herself and the future, she reasoned. She found a beautiful matching plum-colored shoe with the wedge heel that she liked. The heel said that she was an administrator and not a teacher or yard duty, but it wasn't so high or narrow so that she couldn't run after a potential wayward student if she needed to. Besides, she loved the authoritative sound that her shoe made as she walked down the hallway, naturally reminding people that she was, in fact, the boss. She had Monday covered in terms of attire, but would she be able to dress for Tuesday without another trip back to Fashion Island, she wondered. If she absolutely had to shop some more, she would. After all, she was the kind of employee who always went the extra mile and would do whatever it took, even if that meant going back to the high-end retail stores until she had exactly what she needed.

When she got to Harbor Street Elementary, Kat, Ms. Anderson that is, was already waiting for her, ready to show her the ropes. Sofia instinctually checked out Ms. Anderson's attire, as an added effort to self-assess her own wardrobe choices and make sure that her clothing choices fit the climate here in southern California. That was one thing that her experience had taught her along the way, that each region, town, and community had its own culture and she wanted to look like she was a part of it, which meant taking a moment to compare the attire to that of the other employees in administrative roles. The first thing Sofia noticed about Ms. Anderson was what her ensemble said about her, and Ms. Anderson's outfit said that she was professional, conservative, and no-nonsense. There was nothing flashy about Ms. Anderson, no proverbial bells and whistles in the way she accessorized, it was just the basics, no more, no less. In fact, there were no accessories that Sofia could identify—no earrings, makeup, or jewelry to speak of. No scarf where a necklace may have been, just a small black purse to hold a minimal amount of belongings: keys, glasses, and her favorite bleach pen for emergencies. *I bet the inside of her purse is super organized*, Sofia mused. Instead, Sofia noticed that she wore a sensible pants suit, high-quality shoes, and a dark blazer in a smart, conservative color. This was useful information for Sofia, who was just getting to know Ms. Anderson. Sofia hoped that her own observations would be clues to help her work well with Ms. Anderson as she used her observations to make some judgments: Ms. Anderson was the type of superintendent who would be calm, professional, and most importantly,

"stay in her lane." Sofia found this to be both intimidating and a relief, as she had worked for other bosses who would explode at the drop of a hat. Sofia liked the vibe she was picking up from Ms. Anderson and was hoping that she would be able to live up to her expectations.

After showing Sofia to her new office, Ms. Anderson (she told Sofia to call her Kat) walked Sofia through the school so she could meet her staff and get the lay of the school. It was a relatively small school in southern California, with just 12 teachers, including one special education teacher, several aides and yard duties, a secretary, and an attendance clerk. The school nurse was only there on Tuesdays, Sofia learned, as she worked at the other school sites in the district the rest of the week. The same was true for the occupational therapist, speech pathologist, and psychologist. After making the rounds and touring the school, Sofia began to get settled. She found her office which was in total disarray and devoid of decor, which she set out to clean up immediately. If she was going to be effective as an administrator, her office had to be at least functional, although Sofia was hoping for a little inspiration.

When Sofia finally left work at 5:30 Monday evening, she was half-starved and totally drained mentally. The hardest thing about taking a new job was learning all the names, where things are located, new policies and procedures. Keeping it all in her head made her feel as though she was drinking information out of a fire hydrant, rather than the slow trickle of information that her brain could digest. As she pulled onto the bridge to go back to her house, she decided to stop at the Balboa Island Market to pick up some things (was she out of wine?) for dinner. As much as she had wanted to end her day by walking down to the bay to immerse her feet in the soft sand and water, it was dark at 5:30 and so she would have to wait until May and beyond when it stayed light longer. For now, she would settle for takeout sushi and a glass (or maybe two) of wine. She could sit comfortably on her sofa, crack open a window, and listen to the lull of the waves outside instead. As she opened up the bottle of wine, a tired smile crept across her face, as she realized she had accomplished her dream. She was now officially working and living on Balboa Island. As she sat on her couch and felt so satisfied with everything, it wasn't long before she nodded off to sleep, with her window open, and her front door unlocked. Little did she know, her neighbor Duke, was on his couch next door, doing the exact same thing, minus the wine.

It was fortunate that Balboa felt so safe. As a young girl who used to vacation there every year, it was one of the reasons the island had felt so idyllic. Back home her house had been burglarized, three times to be exact, during the day. She had lived in a middle-class neighborhood that was nicer than most of her friends, but this was the kind of thing that happened and was the reason that the doors always had to be locked. Whether it was true or not, the feeling she had on Balboa as a kid, was that everyone was so happy here, and so friendly, that no one would ever do anything bad to anyone ever. Furthermore, everyone seemed so rich on Balboa that why would anyone ever need to take anything? Now that she was older, she knew this wasn't true. But the feeling of peace and safety and happiness had lasted until adulthood. It was one of the many reasons she had wanted to return to her place of happy memories following her traumatic divorce from Ned.

Chapter 14 - Duke

As was common in most crowded cities and definitely southern California, housing was at a premium which meant that they were built close to one another. And with the weather and beach both being elements from outside that people wanted to bring in, it meant that windows were open, neighbors were close to one another, and there was noise. And as he lay sleeping on his couch like he did most nights (why did he even have a bed?), with the windows open and the door ajar for his cat Bonkers, he heard a noise unfamiliar to him. The noise itself wasn't unfamiliar; it sounded like someone was snoring...but who? He looked at the five empty beer bottles that lay on the ground next to the couch where he had fallen asleep, and quickly scanned his brain to recall the events from the night before. *There wasn't...no...couldn't be...no, hold on a second...what was I doing last night? Did I...noooooo, did I bring home a girl? Is there someone in my bed...snoring?* He knew he had had some wild nights lately, but surely he'd remember that... He couldn't remember. *No, wait hold on a second,* he thought...

As he stood up his foot caught the top of a beer bottle and it rolled beneath him. He tried to catch his balance but there were so many bottles below him that his other foot came down and his toe got stuck. "AWWWWWWWW fuck shit!" he yelled. "What the fuck!" Without thinking, he swung his foot that had the beer bottle stuck to it, and it flew across the living room and right into a window that instantly shattered into pieces. The sound of the broken glass reverberated throughout the small room, and he screamed again when his foot came down on a shard. "God

Dammmmmnnitt!" he yelled at the top of his lungs. It soon became evident, now that he was fully awake, that the snoring was not some bimbo he had brought home from the night before, but snoring from next door.

Sofia arose with a start and grabbed her empty wine bottle, holding it like a baseball bat ready to swing at the intruder, or commotion, or whatever it was going on. *Was it a f'ing party?*

At this time of night? On a Monday? Didn't these mother truckers know that she had work in the morning? Her happy and safe feeling that being on this island brought had now been vanquished. Her pulse and heartbeat were pounding and her adrenaline was through the roof. She was ready for a fight. She ran out of the house, wine bottle ready to strike, and looked wildly in every direction.

She couldn't see. It was dark. She stood there for another moment, trying to figure out what the noise had been that had jolted her out of her sleep. And then she saw him. He was tall, dark, and handsome. And he was bleeding. He was also standing there too, smiling, not saying a word. When she finally got her wits about her and realized she was being watched by Mr. Model, whatever his name was, she became hugely embarrassed and quickly brought the wine bottle down to her side. *Would I be able to play this off by acting casual?* she wondered. Nope. Too late. All

Sofia could do was take a breath in and try not to die...

When she finally collected herself, she looked down at his foot and noticed the blood. "Are you okay?" she asked. "What happened?"

Ever the gentleman, (at least for the moment or in front of a pretty lady), Duke decided not to go through the sordid details of how her snoring had caused this series of unfortunate events that led them to both be standing, half-naked, in the dark, on their patios with the two-foot-tall picket fences that separated them. "Bad dream..." he said. "I need to learn to pick up after myself more...I can be such a slob at times. Hey, I'm really sorry for waking you, especially at this ungodly hour. Maybe we can chat sometime over dinner, when, uh, I don't have blood all over myself?" "All right, sure," Sofia said. She pointed to his foot."Need some help with that?" She let out a sly smile. "I know that people sometimes crush grapes with their feet, but I'm pretty sure they remove the bottle first..."

"Very funny," he replied. "For your information, this was beer, not wine. No grapes were harmed during the incident. And no, I will take care of it, the blood, that is. But thanks for the offer. Again, I apologize for scaring you. Goodnight."

As he walked back to his house he thought about Sofia. He guessed she was a good 20 years older than him, at least. He didn't know much about her other than she seemed to live alone.

As a new neighbor that had moved in, he thought it would be nice to make amends. And no, for once, he wasn't trying to get into her pants.

Not that she wasn't attractive, he thought, but it was mid-February, and for New Year's his friends had made him a bet that he couldn't "just be friends" with a woman. And up until now, they had been correct. But the more he thought about it, he realized, maybe it was time that he grew up a bit and proved to himself, not just his friends, that he could have a relationship with a woman. A relationship, unlike his other female friendships, that wasn't about sex.

Chapter 15 - Valerie

Valerie couldn't believe what she was hearing. How could this be happening? Pancreatitis? What was pancreatitis? Unfortunately, Valerie had a sinking feeling that she was about to find out. According to her doctor, pancreatitis was caused by gallstones or heavy alcohol consumption. It was a problem with the enzymes in which they would try to digest the pancreas. This was easy enough to understand. But what Valerie didn't understand were the lifestyle changes that were recommended in order to prevent a recurrence. The other piece of this that didn't make sense to Valerie was that this condition was more common in middle-aged and elderly people. None of this made sense, as Valerie took impeccable care of herself. How would she be able to adjust her lifestyle when she already did everything right? Did her doctor even have the right diagnosis? She made a mental note to ask Char what she could find out about this doctor the next time she spoke to her. She then decided, since she was going to be stuck in this hospital bed for a while, that she would text Char to thank her for saving her and bringing her into the hospital.

"Hi, Char Char...how are you? Turns out I have pancreatitis. I wanted to let you know because I know the hospital won't tell you anything. Not sure how long I will be here. Thank you so much for being such a great friend! I owe you! If you can take care of Gus for me until I get back, I would really appreciate it. Love you, friend! -Val"

Char was sound asleep and pinned down with Gus squarely on top of her, having some sort of a dog dream, when her phone beeped, notifying her of a new text. As she couldn't move and didn't want to disturb Gus, she felt around the bed until her hand felt her cell. She picked it up and read her text from Valerie. *Pancreatitis? Wow,* she thought. Her poor friend. Although she knew next to nothing about pancreatitis, her friend's text indicated that she would be held up at the hospital for at least a few more days. "Looks like you and I will be spending some quality time together, big buddy," she said. Gus lifted his face, opened his eyes, and gave her a big, wet lick right across her face and lips.

"Ooooooh!" she squealed. "Gus!" She then typed a quick text back to Val:

"Oh, Val! You poor thing! I am so sorry. Of course I will take care of Gus! Please let me know if you need anything! Get better! Love you too! - Char"

Valerie wondered if her friend thought she was off the hook with the workouts, now that she was laid up in the hospital. *No way,* she thought to herself, *she's my friend and I am going to help her. It is not about the money. Anyway, I am going to need something to take my mind off things and give me something to do while I am here. I will text her daily with her workouts, and she can let me know how she is doing. I don't think she has any idea how much this will actually help me. Right now I need a diversion, something positive and uplifting to get my head out of this hospital and my ailments.*

Valerie was a staunch believer in the mind and body connection, and she knew she would have to find a way to stay positive in order to get back on her feet. She remembered the story that

Char had told Valerie about Valerie's friend, Sofia, the one who had the twins. Apparently, when Sofia had been pregnant, she had initially been extremely happy by the news, as she had desperately wanted children and had several miscarriages. But after a while, as the pregnancy continued, Sofia started having anxiety that was really bad. She couldn't stop thinking about all the "what ifs" of motherhood. *What if I don't get any sleep? What if I can't handle twins? What if they are premature? What if I go crazy?* According to Char's story, Sofia couldn't escape these thoughts, and as the pregnancy went on, the thoughts grew worse and worse. She simply couldn't turn them off.

"Try not thinking about a pink elephant right now," Sofia had said to Valerie. "What did you just do?" Clearly, Valerie had pictured a pink elephant. And so it was with thoughts...and blood pressure. The more stressed out you are, the higher the blood pressure. In the end, Sofia's bad thoughts had almost caused the worst to happen: she ended up with pre-eclampsia (the hallmark of which is high blood pressure) and delivered the twins two months early. Her heart had been failing, her lungs had filled with fluid, and she was too sick to even have a C-section. In the end, everyone turned out okay, but not everyone in her situation was so lucky. *No,* thought Valerie, *I am going to remain positive. I am going to distract my mind from this by focusing on my passion.*

Helping my friend, she resolved, *will ultimately help me. And with everything going on in this world right now, couldn't we all benefit from a little positivity?*

Chapter 16 - Sofia

By now several weeks had passed by and winter was slowly turning into spring. Well, at least on the calendar, anyway. Being in southern California, this typically meant exchanging a light coat for a sweatshirt, or a sweatshirt for a cardigan over short sleeves. The truth was, the weather didn't really change all that much on Balboa Island, and the lack of a serious cold spell and frost meant that the trees never turned those vibrant crimson colors with varying shades of red, orange, and yellow like they did in other climates. Other than it being a little cooler with some fog, there wasn't a huge difference between the seasons. Even summertime often had fog until noon, so summer wasn't that different from spring, and so on and so forth. There was one additional nice fringe benefit of spring, however: Spring Break! And Sofia was really looking forward to it. It would be the first time she could really relax since she had moved to Balboa. How would she spend it? She didn't really know too many people other than those at work, and hanging out with them on her time off didn't really sound too appealing. *Actually,* she thought again, *Kat and I seem to have some things in common, I know she's a self-described "foodie" who likes her wine. Perhaps she would be willing to show me some of the cooler places down here?* So much had changed since she'd spent time here as a kid. She didn't put too much thought into it and began to consider her other options. Should she see if one of her twins, Kevin or Matthew, had some time to come down? She really missed them and would love to spend some time with them. She resolved right then and there to give them a call and see what plans they had. Perhaps they could even go to Disneyland, but she would have to look to see if it was even open right now with Covid and all... And then she remembered her other news she would have to tell them when she called: they hadn't yet seen or known she had gotten a tattoo. Surely they would think their mom was cool getting a tattoo, right? As it turned out, Sofia was so, so wrong.

"Oh my god, Mom, seriously?" Matthew, who was two and a half hours older than his brother, had said over the phone. "Really? Why? What's wrong with you? You are too old for
    that."

Okaaay... she considered. *Perhaps Matthew was the wrong son to start with.* So next, she tried with Kevin.

"Mom, I am not trying to judge you or anything," Kevin said, "But first you and dad got divorced, then you moved down to Balboa...and now you got a tattoo? Are you going through some kind of mid-life crisis or something?"

Alrighty then... Sofia thought, reaching for what was left of the wine in the open bottle.

Perhaps they weren't as ready for that as I had hoped... As she finished her wine, she thought about what they had said and wondered, was she? Was she going through a midlife crisis? She decided they were just shocked at the changes their mom had made. As she tried to look at her life in retrospect, she thought about how her confidence had grown through the years, and yes, she thought, she had become less conservative as well as time had passed. Not only had she been openminded about many contemporary issues, but she had finally broken down and got herself her first tattoo. *Yep,* she laughed, *I've really gone off the deep end now!*

Next Sofia rethought her vacation plans, as both her boys had work commitments and were not going to be able to visit just now. Perhaps over the summer, they had said. Sofia certainly hoped so.

Impulsively, the next day at work, Sofia mentioned to Kat that perhaps they could hang out over the break. Sofia wasn't sure, but she thought that Kat was single and had never heard her talking about any children, only something about a Jake and an Annie, which Sofia thought she had overheard that they were her cats. *The worst thing she can say is no,* thought Sofia.

The next day at work, as she and Katrina were finishing up a budget meeting and heading back to their respective offices, Sofia decided to pop the question.

"Hey, I was wondering, if you don't already have plans during the break, perhaps you wouldn't mind showing me around a bit? I used to spend so much time here as a kid, but a lot has changed since then. I'd really love to check out some of the new shops, and restaurants, that is, if you are up to it?"

Surprisingly, Kat had agreed. *Great!* Sofia smiled. She would not have to be alone over her vacation, and she could see some new sights besides. Sofia also hoped there was a winery within driving distance, as she could really use some more wine and loved the experience of tasting the wine as opposed to just going to the grocery store and bringing something home. Going to the winery, selecting the perfect bottle, making a day of it, all became part of the experience when she later added it to her collection. Each bottle represented another memory. Memories she would soon have with Kat.

Chapter 17 – Duke

"Knock, knock!" Sofia could hear Duke yelling to her through the partially opened front door. "Sofia, you home? I was wondering if you wanted to have...dinner?" Duke had apparently caught Sofia getting out of the shower, and when she heard someone at the front door, she had thrown a towel around herself and added one to her head as well. She was still dripping from head to toe and was lucky she didn't slip trying to run to the door. "Hey! Careful!" Duke said, "You're lucky you didn't slip!"

"Um...thank you, Captain Obvious..." *Why am I flirting with him?* she kept wondering.

He was half her age and she didn't even like his type. In fact, she didn't know what "type" she liked anymore. After her marriage to Ned, she had just wanted someone she could be happy with...a happy person to be with her in her happy place. The happy place had been a lot easier to find than the happy person, but seeing Duke standing in front of her definitely put a smile on her face, although she wasn't exactly sure why. Maybe it was because he was so gorgeous, in a younger, beach bum sort of way. Maybe it was because she was lonely and needed a friend, or maybe it was because he was now standing in her doorway, this time with a full bottle of wine in his hand.

"How's the foot?" she asked.

"Still attached to my ankle," he said. "I know, I'm 'Captain Obvious' after all. I need to come up with some better material. You're smart anyway. Didn't you say you were a principal? I didn't think principals drank wine...or got tattoos," he added, admiring her ankle. "I always had this image of them growing up when I was called to their office as a kid of them being so prim and proper."

"Yes," she replied. "Most of them are, especially when they are calling you into their office," she said. "And my guess is you weren't exactly being called in for a reward, or were you?" "Right," he said with a smile, "not exactly. Anyway, I was hoping you would have dinner with me tonight. After last night's fiasco, I kind of wanted to make it up to you. And besides, you are the new neighbor here and I haven't exactly been over, well, neighborly. Since we are going to be living within snoring distance, I thought it might be best to get to know one another a bit. I have a barbecue and can throw on some chicken if you like chicken... You look like you eat chicken, not that you wouldn't enjoy a nice steak..." He was rambling. *Why am I rambling? I'm not at the radio station having another solo hour of talk radio for Pete's sake!*

"Yes," she said, "I would love to join you for dinner. What did you say we were having?" She looked down at her attire of two towels. *Well, at least they match,* she thought, embarrassed. And with that, she closed the door and went inside to find something suitable to wear to dinner. Sofia had settled for a simple tube-style dress with no straps. It was blue, and originally she wore it as a too-long skirt, but lately, she rather enjoyed how comfortable it was to just pull it up over her chest and wear it as a dress. *One less article of clothing to put on and wash,* she thought. Besides that, with this "dress" she enjoyed the freedom of not having anything tight around her waist. She had always hated that, and avoided pants and shorts as much as possible, preferring to wear loose-fitting clothes around her waistline. She had always felt feminine in a dress, and with little to coordinate except a pair of flip-flops, it was a win-win in the fashion department. Sofia acknowledged that she wasn't interested in Duke anyway since he seemed like a stereotypical beach bum type, so she was comfortable showing up for dinner dressed casually. Duke had on a clean, white, v-neck style t-shirt, khaki shorts, and leather flip-flops. Already Sofia was impressed, as she had never seen Duke in an actual shirt. She wasn't even sure he owned one. Then again, she decided that would explain why the shirt was so clean. He's probably never worn it before. Or better yet, he probably just opened it out of one of those plastic packages that undershirts come in. And as for the food, that had been a pleasant surprise as well, as Duke had expertly grilled two chicken breasts in a pineapple teriyaki marinade, complete with a green salad and French bread. And of course, there was wine. And beer, for Duke.

As she lay in bed that night, Sofia thought about what a pleasant evening she had had getting to know Duke. It was nice to know she had a man next door that she could count on in case of an emergency, not that she wasn't capable by herself. It was just that being new to living on the island, it was comforting to know that she had a friend...*was he a friend?* Maybe not quite friend status yet, she acknowledged, but a neighborly acquaintance! Yes, he was a neighborly acquaintance with potential for...friendship. Not only had she enjoyed the opportunity to sit outside and relax, but it was also good to have someone local to talk to. It made her feel more settled in her community. And she had been pleasantly surprised at how easy he was to talk to, moving from one subject to another with much ease and having much knowledge. She wondered what he did for a living. An attorney, perhaps? A journalist? Lobbyist? *Who knows,* she thought; perhaps he was even a professional surfer. Regardless, he certainly had left an impression. And after their first real meeting in the middle of the night, half-naked, with blood on his foot, this impression had been much, much better. This is why Sofia thought it was especially odd that as she drifted off to sleep, she realized her thoughts had turned to Kat, her boss.

If Sofia's thoughts had been about work and subsequently turned to Kat, that would have been one thing. This, however, was different. She started wondering about Kat on a personal level. *Why is Kat single? Has she ever been married?* Sofia found her independence appealing and her successful position as a superintendent super sexy! Who was this independent transplant from Ohio that had found herself leading a well-performing district in southern California? For the first time in her entire life, Sofia began to imagine what it would be like to kiss...not Duke, but another woman.

Chapter 18 - Char

"Guuuuussss! Wait up!" Char yelled as Gus pulled her around the perimeter of the island on their morning walk, which had become a new routine for them. Something else that had become part of the routine was Gus's insistence that he drag Char as fast as her legs would go around the island. Never mind that there were seniors and toddlers out on walks of their own, travelers going for a stroll, and a myriad of people just stopped in the middle of the sidewalk, sipping coffee or greeting one another. Gus was going full steam ahead, so happy and so strong! *How was he this strong?* she wondered. Surely Valerie could just loan him out to give people a good workout. Never mind going to the beach and doing a formal workout routine when you could walk Gus...for free! Since Valerie had been in the hospital with pancreatitis, she and Gus had become quite the pair. Sometimes Char even felt like Valerie must have been somehow inside Gus in spirit, willing Gus to push Char to work out harder and harder, faster and faster...go!...go!...go! Char knew her friend well enough to know that it wouldn't be beneath her to try to motivate her even from her hospital bed and do everything she could to help her reach her goal to get in shape and be fit. Not to mention, she would help her to fit back into the skinny jeans that she loved and had paid a small fortune for...

As Char blazed past the other walkers and strollers, her mouth went on autopilot as she gasped, "Whoops, sorry! Excuse us...so sorry...whoops...Guuuuus!" She received a few dirty looks from some annoyed couples, while most tried not to laugh at the comedic sight. Gus was just so darn happy! And Char, by contrast, was...horrified! She was afraid they would get tangled up on another person, knock over a child or older person, or that she wouldn't be able to stop when they came to a road, as Gus would just keep going. No matter what she did, Gus just pulled harder and harder, literally dragging her around the island. How many laps would he take her around the island? If her memory served her correctly, one loop around the island was about three miles...if this kept up, she would be up to nine miles without even knowing what happened. *Thanks, Val,* she thought sarcastically, knowing full well that Valerie could not have predicted this.

Char decided that when she made it back home, she would shower and call the hospital to see how Valerie was doing. She felt so bad for her friend, who was such a sweet, kind person but just couldn't seem to catch a break. It seemed as though it would be so easy to despair right now, particularly if she was in Valerie's shoes. Valerie had lost a lucrative job as a gourmet chef due to Covid and had tried to reinvent herself in order to stay on her feet. She turned to her passion, fitness, and had used up the last of her savings and credit card limit to go to school to get her license to qualify as a personal trainer. Just as she accomplished this and had started with Char, her first client, she had gotten sick. And now she lay in the hospital, alone, without anyone to support her, not knowing how she would pay her bills or even if her insurance had already lapsed. Valerie loved her friend so much, and just hoped she would be okay.

After the walk/run, Char dragged herself into the doorway of her house where she dropped down on the floor, breathless. Gus too, finally settled down next to her, as though he had finally come down from the excitement of the run, and promptly fell asleep, still panting. When she was finally able, Char slowly crawled, then walked to the kitchen to get a bottle of water. She limped her way to the shower where she sat down and let the cool water cascade down over her, and slowly began to soap herself, starting with her legs. Assuming she still had enough energy, she hoped to go down to the hospital to see Valerie, even if it meant waving at her through the window while talking on the phone, thanks to Covid. Of course, that would mean getting off the shower floor, getting dressed, and driving down to Hoag Hospital. But there was time for that, later. Instead, she grabbed her towel and wrapped it loosely around herself, crawled down next to Gus, and fell asleep.

Chapter 19 - Katrina

As Katrina stood waiting outside the food court in Fashion Island for Sofia to arrive for their day of shopping, she looked around and admired all of the opulence. From her humble beginnings in Ohio, she had worked her way up to superintendent in trendy Orange County. While the shopping, wine, and fine dining had definitely rubbed off on her over the years, she often still felt a little out of place here, as she didn't consider herself to be one of those girly girls that were all over Orange County and LA, nor did she want to be. She was happy to be spending time with Sofia during her week off for spring break, although she also wanted to protect her job and status and hoped Sofia wouldn't blab to everyone at work about how the two of them had hung out over the weekend. Orange County was so conservative! As Sofia's direct supervisor, she didn't need anyone making "a thing" over the fact that the two of them had spent time socializing over the break. Any bit of gossip would run rampant throughout the workplace, and other employees never needed much reason to become jealous when the boss paid particular attention to one employee over the other. The last thing Kat needed was the head of the teacher's union down her throat, and so she made a point to tell Sofia later on that day that she hoped that their afternoon would be left discreet. Katrina felt a little nervous meeting Sofia today for these reasons. On the other hand, what she did on her off time wasn't anyone's business. She certainly had a right to get together with whomever she chose. Katrina turned around to see Sofia at the precise moment that Sofia came bouncing up from behind, dressed in her cute black boots and black leggings. Although Katrina hardly admitted it even to herself, she did enjoy just being around Sofia, and she was particularly delighted in glancing at Sofia's cute figure, particularly her legs, whenever she got the chance. Of course, her admiration would never be revealed to anyone, but at the same time, Kat couldn't help noticing just how cute Sofia was.

After shopping for a few hours, Katrina found two new pairs of black loafers from Cole Haan, and Sofia found a very feminine dress in pale pink that would be suitable for work. It came up just above the knee and showed off Sofia's best feature, her legs. By this time it was midafternoon and neither had had any lunch. They settled on an outdoor seating area (most indoor dining was closed due to Covid anyway) at a little wine bar that served various charcuterie along with small appetizers. It was a typical southern California day, which meant that the weather felt absolutely perfect. It was warm with a soft ocean breeze, blue skies above, and the moisture in the air from the nearby ocean gave a nice cooling sensation on their arms and backsides. By the time they settled down for lunch, Katrina and Sofia were getting to know each other beyond work. Katrina noticed that Sofia was sharing intimate details about her divorce, her childhood summers that were spent in southern California on Balboa, and how she made her dad wait 45 minutes in line with her for the Corkscrew roller coaster at Knott's Berry Farm, only to change her mind about going on it at the last minute. Katrina smiled to herself and wondered why she always seemed to have this effect on people. Was it her high-ranking position as a superintendent? Or did people feel comfortable telling her their life stories for another reason? She simply didn't know, but she decided it was a compliment. For whatever reason, people trusted her. Sofia trusted her, and that felt good because Katrina was really starting to enjoy Sofia's company, even when Sofia got up and excused herself to go to the restroom, and gave Katrina a swift kiss on the cheek as she left. *Okay,* thought Katrina, *that was certainly friendly. Perhaps she is feeling that second glass of wine that she just had and gets overly affectionate (not to mention impulsive) when she drinks?*

"How old are you?" Sofia asked Katrina when she returned.

"Fifty," lied Katrina. Katrina had already crossed a line by spending time with someone she supervises at work, she wasn't about to cross another one and reveal her true age. No, she would have to know Sofia a whole lot better before that happened. But aside from the random kiss on the cheek that Katrina chalked up to nothing but an overly affectionate moment inspired by several strong libations, and asking her about her age, Katrina was having a really good time. She had already decided that Sofia was cute to be around, fun, and bubbly, so getting to have a drink or two with her outside of work and also squeeze in some shopping was definitely worth the risk of "favoring" an employee. She would make a point to talk to Sofia about keeping their weekend get-together low-key once they returned to the office.

The rest of the day continued in much the same way, shopping until they were hungry, eating until they became thirsty, and so on and so forth. Along the way, they continued to talk and share details of their lives, until suddenly it was nearly 8 p.m. Arms weighed down by various shopping bags from Neiman Marcus, Cole Haan, Banana Republic, and Macy's, they found their way to their cars and said goodbye. By both accounts, it had been a perfect day.

"We should hang out again soon," said Sofia, being the more forward one of the two.

"Yes!" Katrina agreed. "I have a wine pickup next weekend in Temecula if you'd like to join me..." she trailed off.

Sofia didn't hesitate before she heard herself responding in the affirmative. "Are you kidding me?" she exclaimed. "I would love to go!"

Chapter 19 - Sofia

One of the benefits of being divorced, Sofia realized early on, was getting to experience things you never experienced during the course of your marriage. For Sofia, this was because her spouse didn't like certain things: watching sporting events, drinking wine, fine dining, or collecting knick-knacks. So simply, they had been off-limits for Sofia. Since Ned didn't care for wine, it wasn't surprising then that he also didn't enjoy wine tasting either. Sofia had always found it intimidating, which was a bit ironic as she was a principal and people often found her intimidating, just based on what she did for a living. The truth of the matter was that Ned had never liked alcohol of any type, which meant she brought home a bottle or two when it went on sale at the grocery store, but nothing much more than that. She certainly wasn't a wine connoisseur by any stretch of the imagination and found people who went to wineries to be, well...sophisticated. So when Katrina offered to take Sofia with her to pick up her wine down in Temecula, Sofia jumped at the chance.

Sofia was ready for work the following Monday and couldn't decide which she was more excited about, to get back to her new job, wear her new pink dress with her long black boots, or talk to Kat about going wine tasting that weekend. *What was going on?* she wondered. She had NEVER, EVER been attracted to, interested in, or even thought about a woman in any way other than strict friendship, and the fact that Sofia was starting to fixate on Kat, and purposely trying to look extra good at work in case she happened to run into her in a meeting, both excited her and troubled her at the same time. On the one hand, she wanted to shake these intrusive thoughts from her head. *What in the world?* she kept asking herself. On the other hand, the thought of flirting with Kat—would she ask Kat to watch her try on clothes the next time they went shopping, just to see what Kat's reaction might be? She envisioned herself taking off her top right at the precise moment she asked Kat to come in to look at her new outfit in the dressing room for some fashion advice and pretending it was an unplanned and embarrassing moment, while she secretly wanted to see what Kat would do. Or what if Sofia opened the dressing room door just enough for Kat to come in, and then closed the door behind her so that they were both in the dressing room together? Sofia would then try on several outfits which would require her to take off all her clothes down to her bra and underwear, and stare at Kat intently to assess her response. Would Kat be flattered? Unable to resist? Would she see her cheeks flush with embarrassment, or possibly arousal? Perhaps Sofia would take advantage of a knowing look, push her against the wall of the crowded changing room and start kissing her, passionately? Would Sofia like the kiss of another woman? Or just as likely, would she be grossed out and regret her actions, and be thankful she got this ridiculousness that had inhabited her thoughts out of her head, once and for all? But what would she say if it backfired? *Way too risky,* she thought. Better to wait until they were drinking, and then she could claim to have not known what she was doing if it backfired. She hoped it wouldn't, but she couldn't be sure. Life was too short, she rationalized. At that moment she knew she was going to find out, sooner rather than later. Yeah, it was risky. Some would even say gutsy, or crazy. She wanted so badly to try it, to know what these new feelings were, and she didn't want anyone to talk her out of it. She decided right then and there that she would attempt something to get her feelings across when they went to Temecula. She also decided she wasn't going to tell a soul. She didn't want anyone stealing her fun and squelching her new curiosity with common sense. *No...I must follow my heart.* She repeated this over, and over, and over, as if each repeat of this mantra would somehow make it easier to do what she knew she shouldn't do, especially with her boss. Her thoughts kept going back to the words of her son when she had told him she got her tattoo...

"...midlife crisis Mom...are you sure? Mom? Mom? Mommmmmm!" Now she wondered, but she didn't care. No, she was free. *Life is too short...life is too short...life is too short...* A second mantra had entered her head. *Follow your heart...life is too short.* The thoughts wouldn't stop. She decided at that moment to put her feelings out there and see where they led. Life WAS too short, after all. Anyway, other than her dignity and job and possibly a roof over her head, what did she have to lose? On the other hand, if it worked out, she stood to gain so much more...true love, and with an unlikely partner, indeed. As she put on the final touches of her makeup, picked up her lunch off the kitchen table, and stepped outside to greet another blissfully beautiful southern California day, she couldn't wait to see what the day would bring. She hoped that she would see Kat and that Kat would notice and like the way she looked again today.

Chapter 20 - Valerie

While Sofia continued to delight in the excitement of the moral dilemma that was growing inside her, Valerie continued to have struggles of her own. Her symptoms had not abated even in the slightest. She was tired of being alone in a hospital bed and struggling to stay positive. She flipped through the news on the TV that was hanging down in front of her, trying to find something to pass the time and take her mind off of her pain. If anything, the television news and the knowledge of what was going on in the country seemed to make her feel worse. She really wondered if things were reaching the end, possibly for her life as well as the country's democracy. People were dying. She felt that her wing of the hospital, with all of its pain and suffering and loneliness, was no different than the world at large. It was all becoming lonely, scary...divisive. After eight years of having an African American president, the country was now more polarized than ever. Anti-American groups such as the Ku Klux Klan and the Proud Boys, (and QAnon...what was QAnon?) had more notoriety than ever before, and the nation seemed poised on the brink of another civil war. Her Christian friends told her that everything that's happening right now: the pandemic, the civil unrest, the threat to our democracy, and all of the negative rhetoric that existed in society at large had all been predicted in the Bible. People were saying that this was the end. We were getting close to the end, just as Valerie was worried that she was getting to the end... *No! No! No!* She fought off these thoughts like the evil they were. Valerie knew how important the mind-body connection was to her healing, and yet she just seemed to be one part of the larger picture. There didn't seem to be anywhere to turn to feel as though things were going to be okay. How could she heal when everything was in disarray and seemed to be dying? There was still no cure for the coronavirus, no vaccine, no nothing. People were tearing down historical statues, there was more violence, race riots...*oh my god. And don't even get me started on global warming,* she thought. She rang her bell for her nurse. She needed something to calm her nerves, to give her the will to get better. Alone in her bed, everything hurt. There was no one by her side, no one to talk to, and all she could do was cry. She felt the teardrop roll down her cheek until it hit her lip, and so she pursed her lips to stop it from running down her chin. There came one salty tear after another. Slowly at first, and then faster, faster, one stream of salty tears turned into two rivers that overflowed, down her cheeks, beyond her chin, down to fill the gully that was her neck, until that too overflowed to her hospital gown. This was not what she needed. This was not helping. And then she sobbed harder, as she realized she had always been strong, and she wondered where that person was and continued to cry as she mourned her. She wanted her stronger, healthier, happier self back. She didn't know how, and right now she needed an escape. She hit the buzzer frantically three more times. *Where is that damn nurse?* she screamed in her head. *Damn it!* And as she cried, her back hurt more. As sad as she was, she was also filled with worry. *Why am I still hurting? What is going on? Why aren't I feeling better? Where is everyone?!* Oh, how she longed for human contact, not with a nurse who was paid to care for her, but from someone she actually loved, who loved her back. She didn't care about Covid exposure, she just needed someone from her family by her side. She couldn't remember the last time she felt so sad or had cried so uncontrollably that she could not only taste her tears but hear herself too. She tried to smother the sounds with her gown, to drown them out. She was embarrassed on top of everything else. She was the one who was positive. She was the one who was strong, physically and mentally. She didn't want to be weak, and now she felt weak in body and spirit. It was all so sad, so wrong.

Chapter 20 - Duke

By contrast, Duke woke up casually late and happy as he always did. The sun was shining, the breeze cool, the waves big. *Oh yeah,* he thought. Not wanting to miss a single moment of this near-perfect day, Duke slung back his black coffee in two huge swigs and threw on a pair of surf shorts, still gritty with sand and slightly damp from the last time he went surfing. He had come home in a rush and had dropped them in a heap on the floor where they lay until now, which is why they were still dirty and hadn't completely dried. This did not bother Duke in the least. He half-heartedly looked around for his flip-flops, and when he didn't see them immediately, abandoned the idea of footwear altogether in exchange for having a few more minutes to enjoy the magnificent weather. Since he no longer needed to look for his shoes, he now decided to look for his keys instead, which he hoped were still sitting in the front seat of his Jeep. He grabbed his surfboard, which was leaning against the side of the house, and was able to secure it in his Jeep in just under 10 seconds. Fortunately, the keys were still there on the passenger's seat, so he didn't need to spend any more time searching his house for them. Instead, he was now in search of the perfect wave, or at least a parking spot not too far from Corona del Mar, one of his favorite surfing spots. As the music blared and the cool air blew through his hair, Duke thought about how lucky he was, and how he couldn't imagine leading a better life than this. He looked at the digital clock that was on the front dashboard of the Jeep. It was 12:15 p.m. He had exactly five hours before work. That meant four hours and 45 minutes to surf, and exactly 15 minutes to rush home, take a quick shower, get dressed, grab some food, and hop back in his...*hmmmmm, okay, I will give myself 20 minutes,* he reconsidered. He was always pushing work to the last second. As a radio host, he knew he couldn't be late. And with the traffic down south, one just never knew. He smiled as he remembered one thing he wouldn't have to do, dry his hair. The wind blowing through the Jeep would take care of that for him, saving him an additional five and a half minutes...

"...Good evening, all you Orange County liberals," Duke laughed at his own joke, "If that was true there would only be three of you out there listening tonight...me, myself, and I..." he continued. "But on a more serious note, the

Covid pandemic is continuing to spread. We cannot continue to believe the lies that are out there, folks." He continued, "I like a good laugh as much as the next guy, but I gotta tell you, this thing isn't getting any better. Social distance, wear your masks, and don't travel anywhere unnecessarily..." Duke was on his first night back on the air since his dinner with Sofia, and he was eager to share,

"All you *Dusk to Dawn* listeners out there...it is time for Duke's 'Whale of A Tale' story that I tell every Thursday night. And tonight's story is sure to get all you naughty boys out there wanting to go back to school, and wishing you would get called into this principal's office...whew!" He hollered and then whistled, all the while playing the canned clapping and cheering complete with cymbals crashing in the background as if there was something to celebrate. "Talk about school fantasies, gentlemen...this hottie at Harbor Street Elementary will have boys begging to get sent to the principal's office and their dads calling for a meeting...and guess what, folks? She lives next door to me! This means I've already seen her right out of the shower and not much else...if you know what I mean...If you want more details gentlemen, I am taking on-air calls right now. Ah," he said, "We already have our first caller...what do you want to know, young sir?" And with that, Duke's segment had once again delivered what his audience had expected, some politics with a splash of raw entertainment thrown in. *A little something for everyone,* he smiled as he drove back home close to dawn.

Duke thought nothing more of it as his Jeep pulled up against the curb outside his house. Another successful night, without having to spend too much of his free time in preparation. While he knew he had embellished his story ever so slightly, he didn't feel the slightest bit guilty about it. The bottom line was that it drove up ratings, gave something salacious to his audience, broke up the mundane news that only covered this awful pandemic, and complemented Sofia. The more he thought about it, the more proud he became of his ability to inform, as well as entertain. He once again threw his keys onto the passenger side of his Jeep, and, deeply satisfied with himself, walked towards his front door. Other than nearly tripping over Bonkers who was lurking in the dark outside the entryway, it had been a perfect day.

Chapter 21 - Char

Char woke to the sound of her cell phone beeping, indicating she had received a text message. She rolled Gus off of her and opened her eyes to see the drool on the ground between the two of them. She then reached up to feel her own cheek, trying to ascertain if the drool had come from her or Gus, or possibly a combination of them both. *Ewwww....gross!* she thought, as she simultaneously wiped her face while attempting to read her text. It was Valerie, with more bad news.

"Hey friend," it began, "looks like I am going to be in here for a bit longer. I still have abdominal pain and fever. The doctors think I may have some sort of infection. I am hoping to come home by the end of the week, but in the meantime, I'm stuck here and unable to take care of

Gus. But what I can do is send you a new workout while I'm here...so here you go..."

Char read on and saw that Valerie wanted Char to do some morning stretches followed by some strength training, a quick run on the beach, no more than 20 minutes, and to try to cool down slowly with a few two-minute planks. Adding Gus to the workout was optional.

"Come on, buddy," she called. "We gotta get up off this floor. We agreed we were going to go down and visit Valerie outside the hospital today. It's already noon and all we've done today is a workout, shower, and sleep." Gus responded by lifting his head ever so slowly off the floor, just enough to see where the noise was coming from, and then, as though an insolent teenager, closed his eyes and went back to sleep, ignoring her completely. "Look here, pal," she addressed Gus, who she knew wasn't listening, "you are the one who dragged me around the island at top speed for three laps, nearly risking my life. You can lay there all you want, but I have no sympathy!

I am getting your leash and we are going to visit Valerie right now... Come on!" she shouted, "Let's go!" Char put the leash on Gus's collar and coaxed him up. "Yep old guy, now you know what it feels like to be dragged! This is what you were doing to me just a bit ago!" As Char tugged at the leash she braced against her right leg, which was already feeling sore from the run just a few hours ago. She wondered how bad it would feel by tomorrow morning, and hoped she would be able to live up to Valerie's expectations. No way was Gus getting out of tomorrow's workout, heck no. "What's good for the goose," she thought, "is good for the gander!"

The odd pair hopped into Char's car and Char rolled down both windows. They drove down the Pacific Coast Highway and let the fresh air work its magic. Before long Gus had perked up and was eagerly poking his head out the window, gulping at the air as they cruised down the road. Char looked over at Gus and quietly giggled to herself. *He is so darn cute! I wonder what he thinks he is chewing—invisible bugs or swallowing air?* Either way, she was starting to enjoy her newfound friend. Not that she had wanted a dog, but considering the circumstances and that it was temporary, Char decided it wasn't so bad having a new workout partner. At the same time, she was worried about Val and hoped she was on the mend. As much as she was enjoying Gus, she wanted Valerie to be okay. As they pulled into the parking lot of the hospital, Char took comfort knowing that soon she would be able to at least see her friend, even if it had to be by standing outside a window.

Gus pulled and jumped and greeted everyone coming in and out of the hospital as Char unsuccessfully tried to restrain him. "Gus!" she repeatedly yelled. "Come on! Stop it!" She knew they could not go inside due to Covid unless you were an employee such as a doctor or nurse, or if you had an appointment. There was even a big sign on the sliding glass doors that read, "NO VISITORS due to the COVID VIRUS. If you need information, please call..." Char stopped to get out her phone so she could find out where Valerie was and wrestled with her purse, car keys, sunglasses, and Gus. Without warning, as a patient was being wheeled out the front entrance, the unruly Gus lunged towards the doors and broke free from Char's weakened grasp. "Oh my God, Gus!" Char screeched. "This is so embarrassing!" Before Char could react, the automatic doors, which had already been closing as Gus raced through, were now closed. Char waited for what seemed like forever for the doors to reopen, which gave Gus valuable seconds to put even more distance between herself and this damn dog. She felt so humiliated! If it weren't for Valerie, at that precise moment she would have left Gus in the hospital and turned around and walked back to her car without him, rather than go inside and have to claim him as her own. *This is precisely why I don't want any children!* she thought. And now she had to suffer the same embarrassment by going in and trying to find this large beast of a dog that was probably scaring all of the patients as well as the hospital staff. *Where the hell is he?* As she walked through the front doors with a frantic look on her face, she was further stopped by the hospital security.

"I'm sorry ma'am, no visitors. There's a sign on the door that says so. I'm going to have to ask you to wait outside."

"But, but, okay, but that...did you see a dog just a few minutes ago? That's my dog! Well, not my dog, but my friend's dog, and, uh..."

"Ma'am, dogs are not allowed in the hospital either," he repeated. "I am going to have to ask that you and your dog leave and go outside immediately or I will have to take further action..." *Oh my God! This asshole!* It was all Char could do to not scream at him right then and there! *What was he thinking? Why wasn't he listening? I don't have time for this bullshit,* she thought. Without thinking a second further, Char started running further into the hospital. She had to get her dog, she had to find him fast and get out of here! She didn't have time to waste with this jerk who clearly wasn't listening! Of course she knew she wasn't allowed in there! Of course she knew Gus wasn't allowed in there either! What was he thinking? Covid or no Covid, dogs simply don't drive themselves down to the hospital and let themselves in to check on patients! Unless you lived under a rock, everyone knew about the damned Covid and the ensuing policies of no visitors!

Char took off as fast as her feet would allow in her flip-flops, which wasn't very fast, and one of them she kept running out of—*damn it!* Disgusted, she finally just picked it up as she ran down the hallway with her flip-flop in her hand, shouting, "Gus! Gus! Gus! Where are you?" She reached the end of the hallway. *Quick, quick, quick,* she thought. *Which way?* She bolted right and rounded the corner, flip-flop in one hand and purse and cell phone in the other when all of a sudden she felt like she had been in a car accident. Something was around the corner and it had halted her while she was running at top speed. Smack! She flew back and felt everything drop from her hands instantaneously as her body hit the hard ceramic floor. Then her head was smacked again as it continued its downward motion, allowing the floor one more strike at her. She lay there still and silent with her eyes closed for just a moment before she willed herself to open her eyes. *What had happened? Had I been in a car accident? No, wait,* she remembered, *I'm in a hospital...hold on...oh yeah, Gus, Valerie...jerk at the front entrance.* It was just like the movies, with her vision coming in and out as she tried to regain focus. It was blurry. And then she saw, standing over her, what she had run into. He was a little over six feet tall with a white lab coat, kind and gentle eyes with a few age lines coming off the sides, and gorgeous, gorgeous dark hair. He was bending over her with his arm outstretched, and he was saying something muffled. It sounded as though he was talking through one of those megaphones, only much, much, quieter and underwater. *If only he would just speak to her normally,* she thought.

When she finally came to, she was in bed, not in her room but in the hospital, with Gus tied to the bed next to her.

Chapter 22 - Sofia

Sofia couldn't remember the last time she had been so angry. *Are you kidding me?* Word had spread like wildfire through her school about the *hot new principal* at Harbor Street Elementary. She was new at the school and trying to establish herself with a positive image, and was mortified when Susan Rumsfield, Cole Carter's mom, had told her about how Duke had described her on his radio show. She was incredulous. *That creep! Ooooooooh! I am so angry I could just scream! I should have trusted my first instinct about that shallow beach bum when I first saw him...Why, he is nothing more than a womanizing, punk loser who was just trying to get me to sleep with him! All this Mr. Nice Guy stuff was nothing more than a ploy to get me in the sack! And to think that I actually was impressed, starting to like him, actually, makes me feel so stupid!*

Why, why, why am I always so damn gullible? I can't believe it! So much for having someone next door that I can count on in an emergency...he better not dare so much as look my way in the future unless he wants a restraining order!

Not that she wasn't flattered, mind you. She would never admit it, but at her age, having a good-looking younger man finds her attractive was an enormous compliment, especially after having been with Ned all those years. But that was so beside the point! The real issue was that as a professional, new to the community, hanging out with someone who spoke of her in this manner made her look like, well, a floozy! It was humiliating! What were all her teachers and parents, not to mention Katrina, going to think of her? Damn him anyway! It was hard enough moving in and establishing yourself, to begin with, and this was the last thing she needed! Now people probably thought she was some sort of beer-drinking lowlife like this Dick...I mean Duke guy next door.

How dare he!

Her next thought was of Katrina, her boss. She better go talk to Katrina immediately, and assure her that she will not be associated with this guy, who she will now refer to as simply "D". Although his real name was Duke, she knew what she meant when she called him D. She will simply explain what happened and that she will not bring shame to the school or the district. She knew how important it was to have a proper image, both on and off campus. In the past, this had never been an issue. Until now. *Thanks, D,* she thought sarcastically. *Thanks a whole fucking lot.* Sofia next took a deep breath, did a quick check in the mirror to make sure she looked okay, and decided to go find Katrina. She hoped it wasn't too late to tell Katrina what had happened before the news had already reached her. At this point, she had a lot to lose, as she not only enjoyed Kat as her boss but was also beginning to feel drawn to her in a unique way, in a way she had never felt about any woman before, ever.

As she marched over to find Kat, she tried to think about what it was, exactly, that drew her to her. Why did she always primp before she saw her, make sure she wore her cutest outfits around her, and want Kat to notice her in a way she had never thought about having another woman notice her before? This was certainly...different.

She arrived at the door to Kat's office and redirected her thoughts back to being angry. She sure hoped Kat wouldn't be in the middle of a meeting or some other engagement that would prevent her from talking to her right then and there. This was so utterly maddening!

The door opened and there was Kat, standing there, wearing her usual dark blazer and khakis that made her look so authoritative and business-like, and dare she say, sexy? *Stay focused...stay focused,* she willed herself. But before she could get out a single word, Kat gave her a sympathetic look that seemed to say, "I know and I understand," all with non-verbal cues. Just being in her calm presence made Sofia feel relieved.

Thank God, she thought to herself. "Kat," she attempted to explain, "you have to know, this is not me. I hardly know this guy and..."

"Do you like him?" Kat asked without warning.

Wait...what? "No, of course not! I hate him! He is such a jerk! He, he, he..." she stammered. She certainly was not expecting this question. Kat swooped in again with just the right words, intuitively knowing how to make Sofia feel better.

"Then don't worry about it. Look, as a principal, you know people are going to stab you in the back from time to time. Let it go. As a superintendent, I've seen all kinds of people. You don't need to worry. I can already tell what kind of a person you are. If I didn't believe in you, I wouldn't have hired you. Besides, everyone who has lived in Orange County for any length of time has heard Duke's Dusk to Dawn segment on the radio and knows he uses inflammatory language to boost ratings." Then Kat changed the subject. "Why don't we go visit that winery in Temecula this weekend? It will take your mind off things."

Sofia smiled and nodded, relieved, in silent agreement. The idea of spending a day with Kat at a winery, away from work, sounded great. As Sofia turned to walk back down the hallway towards her office, Kat called after her. "Don't feel too bad, Sofia," she said with a smile, "Although he didn't say it well, Duke was right. You are a beautiful person, Sofia, inside and out.

Too bad he will never get to know you now the way I will."

As Sofia lay in bed that night, she thought about her day. It had been a day of high highs and low lows. Duke was the lowest low, the rage he stirred up inside her and the worry he brought to her reputation. Katrina, by contrast, was the highest of highs. She loved who she was in her presence. And for the first time in her life, she didn't care that this would make her have to consider a label that she herself had never considered herself to be. She knew people would label her gay, bi, or lesbian...or plain weird. People would judge her, gossip about her, and make her the subject of their conversations. And she was freaking out about being called a hottie, and a good-looking babe by D?

The fact of the matter was that this feeling inside her was so magical, so special, and so unexpected that it felt quite frankly, spiritual. All of a sudden the laws of the universe, how she was *supposed* to be, how to fit into society, what she was taught to believe, simply didn't matter. What she felt was deeper than all of that. It felt so beyond the laws of the physical world that she could almost pity the people who had never experienced this, and were bound to unhappy or mediocre lives based on societal expectations and a lack of bravery. She didn't want her reputation to be destroyed by some punk, some insensitive radio talk show host, because he wasn't worth it. But to be free to follow her deepest self and explore these new and surprising feelings of love toward Kat? This mattered so much that she was willing to risk everything. This was more real than anything she could have imagined for herself, and had ever felt ever before. She was a good girl. She had followed the rules. Girls were supposed to grow up and marry boys, after all. If that was the case, what did this mean? It meant she was brave enough to allow these feelings to emerge, she was brave enough to explore them, to see if they were one-sided or not.

Sofia never could have imagined feeling this way. But on the other hand, wasn't that precisely what these feelings had started with, her imagination? After all, she had been lying down one day when *poof!* these strange and unexpected thoughts had just popped into her head, like a dream that she wanted to hold on to, even as she awoke. And the more she followed her imagination, her gut, and explored them, the more these feelings seemed to be authentic and the path to true happiness, rather than doing what everyone had always wanted her to do, which was to live according to everyone's expectations for her. This was such a powerful place to be! To be in touch with one's inner self, listening to her spirit, which was vastly bigger and more beautiful than limiting herself to society's norms. Suddenly, the connection of her soul with another wasn't dependent on something as temporary as the physical body, as this was much deeper than that. No, she knew something truly unique and special was happening to her, and suddenly it didn't matter if this other person had a penis, a vagina, or a horn between her eyes...it was the connection that mattered. And at the end of the day, at the end of our personal road, isn't that what we are all looking for?

Chapter 23 - Valerie

Valerie was lying in her hospital bed, trying to get comfortable, when she heard the commotion. There had been a ruckus in the hallway that sounded unlike any commotion she had heard in the hospital thus far. There had been screaming and running, and then a large crash. It sounded like someone was trying to escape. She thought she had even heard heavy breathing, panting even...was there a dog loose in the hospital? Maybe one of the transients from outside the hospital, or even someone from the psych ward, she thought. She was curious and waited for an orderly to attend to her so she could ask what happened.

"Oh, I don't know exactly," said the orderly distractedly. "Something about some homeless woman, probably wandering around near the beach, who came up with her dog. Very strange. I think it has been handled though." The orderly then continued tidying up the room and was turning to leave when they both heard the loud barking from down the hall.

"Oh my god!" Valerie said out loud. "Did you hear that? I'm pretty sure there's still a dog here!" She collected herself and cleared her throat. "Could you...I mean, would you mind, um, well, uh, I just have this weird feeling. That 'homeless woman' you mentioned, the one with the dog? Well, my friend was going to come by the hospital and check on me today, and she never made it. And now that I hear that dog barking, I have this weird feeling."

The orderly now gave Valerie her full attention, and she stopped folding the sheet she was working on and turned to face Valerie directly. "Are you trying to tell me that the homeless lady who got in here earlier today is your friend? The one with the dog who tried to attack Dr. Kelley?"

Oh no, oh no, oh no, Valerie thought, horrified. *Gus? Attack someone? No, no, this can't be. There has to be some kind of mistake,* she thought. *Not her Gus! Now what? Quick, think fast...um...oh my god, oh my god, oh my god...*

Okay, okay, okay, just hold on a second here, she thought, trying to calm herself. *They described this woman as homeless, and Char definitely wasn't homeless. A little ripe perhaps, especially after her workouts, but no...this couldn't be. There was obviously some sort of mistake.* She was not going to be on the hook for Gus attacking the head doctor...

"Is this YOUR dog?" Suddenly Gus bounded into the hospital room, and as soon as he saw Valerie, he beelined for her and began wiggling his hind end and licking her incessantly, all the while his tail desecrating the sanitized medical instruments that were ready for use. Two or three various sizes of scissors and tweezers fell off the instrument tray and onto the floor. Gus then stepped on them, adding further insult to the situation.

Valerie took a long, slow, deep breath before considering her response. By the way Gus fawned over her, however, she felt she had little choice but to come clean with the truth. "Gus, Gus!" she uttered. "How did you get in here? What are you doing here?"

As the question was obviously one that Gus couldn't answer, the nurse that had brought him in answered on his behalf. "I looked at his collar and it had your phone number on it. I entered it into our computer and the phone number that I entered matched your name. Is he yours?"

Valerie choked before attempting to answer in the affirmative. She saw visions of dollar signs floating in front of her eyes. Hospital bills, lawyer fees, and now defending herself against who knows what, thanks to Gus. She couldn't believe he had attacked her doctor. Although Valerie tried with all her might to answer a simple "Yes, he's mine," the words simply wouldn't come out.

Instead, she heard herself say instead, "I'd like another Xanax...now please?"

Chapter 24 - Duke

Duke was trying to figure out what went wrong as he lay on his surfboard waiting for the next swell to roll in. He was one of three other surfers waiting for the next ride into shore. It was his day off, and the surfing was dismal thus far. Where were the waves today? As he sat there waiting, he was also just thinking. Waiting, and thinking. Thinking, and waiting. Actually, it was more like perseverating, as he couldn't stop thinking about it. He just didn't get it. He was nearing 30 and was starting to believe he was never going to understand women. He had tried so hard to be kind to Sofia and thought that they had had a really nice evening the other night. He was working on himself, trying to be less shallow, and prove not only to his buddies but to himself that he could be friends with a woman. He respected Sofia. He liked her. She was accomplished, fun, and easy to talk to. She was clearly independent and brave, as she had moved to Balboa Island on her own and found a job, a good job. They had had a nice evening, and he didn't even try to put the moves on her, not that he wouldn't have liked to.

Apparently, it wasn't the evening where the screw-up had occurred. Yes, she was attractive, and even though he had been respectful, he had noticed her sex appeal. He had complimented her on the air and guess he hadn't thought it through first. But what was there to think through? Don't women like being complimented? At least every woman he had ever known had, until now. He honestly thought he was off to a great start until this. This is precisely why he was so shocked when she stormed over after work yesterday and banged relentlessly, and loudly, on his door for 10 minutes before giving up. His neighbor watched her then march back to her house, go inside, and return moments later with a piece of paper, which she then shoved under his door:

"Duke -

Perhaps you are nothing more than a shallow beer-drinking bum after all. Your objectification of me was uncalled for and humiliating. I was glad to have you as a neighbor and possible friend, but not now. I am a human being, not merely fodder for your stupid radio show.

Leave me alone. I regret our time together and want nothing further to do with you, ever. - Sofia"

Chapter 25 - Katrina

Katrina was struggling. She was looking forward to her weekend at the winery for more than she normally would. And it wasn't just because she was going to get more wine, nor was it because she had someone to go with. No, there was one reason she was so elated, and one reason alone: Sofia. It was inappropriate, and she knew it. So she tried to deny how she was feeling, even to herself. She simply had to stop thinking about Sofia, for so many reasons, the least of which was that she was Sofia's boss. Even spending extra time with an employee, no matter how innocent it was, was subject to criticism and accusations of favoritism. And Katrina didn't even completely know what her feelings were, because she was sure that Sofia preferred men anyway. Hadn't she only recently gotten divorced? Although Katrina viewed herself as open-minded, she had always been with men with a few brief exceptions. One was a girlfriend she met through a mutual friend, and the other was a one-night hookup that never went beyond 3 a.m. But there was something different, and special, about Sofia. Still, she reasoned, it didn't matter. She was Sofia's boss and so no matter how much her interest in Sofia was piqued, she would never let it show outwardly.

But that still didn't stop her from smiling when she was around Sofia and being caught up in every moment with her.

Katrina woke up on Saturday morning around 6 a.m., fed her cats, and religiously drank her two and a half cups of coffee before hopping in the shower to get ready to meet Sofia. Temecula was a good hour to two hours from Balboa, depending on the traffic. Katrina glanced out the window and noticed that the weather was overcast and foggy. Although she typically ran warm, she decided to bring a denim-colored jean jacket in case she needed it. She was hoping the fog would burn off and they would get to enjoy a day filled with sunshine.

Katrina spent the next couple of hours cleaning up the house. Before she left, she grabbed two water bottles, one for her and one for Sofia. At the last minute, she grabbed a thin green blanket and threw it in the car as well, just in case. She seemed to recollect that Sofia was often cold, and she prided herself on being thoughtful. Sofia, who also lived on Balboa, was just around the corner, as everything on the island was close together. Katrina pulled up outside Sofia's house precisely at 10 a.m. and was about to get up and walk up to Sofia's door when Sofia appeared.

Katrina couldn't stop the smile that washed over her face as she greeted her. "Morning! How are you doing?" She then glanced to the left and saw a house with a Jeep parked out front with a sandy surfboard in it, and a front door partially opened. "Is that D's house?" she asked. "Want me to slash his tires or steal his surfboard or something? Or better yet, I could run over it, and break it into two pieces!"

Sofia laughed. She appreciated the gesture and could tell by the look on Katrina's face that she wasn't serious. Still, it would have been nice. She really was starting to hate that guy! "No, let's just get going," she said. "I'm looking forward to a nice day, one that doesn't involve anyone whose name begins with the letter D!" Sofia climbed into Katrina's car, and the two of them headed toward the bridge that led off the island, the one that was lined with the colorful flags and storefronts, and various residents who were strolling along with their coffees and cinnamon rolls.

It was going to be a great day, and Sofia was just as excited as Katrina.

The day was going well, and as they drove they talked easily and enjoyed one another's company. It was amazing how much they had to talk about and could roll effortlessly from one topic of conversation to another. They pulled up at Thornton Winery in Temecula around noon, and easily found a parking spot, due to Covid which had limited the number of people who could visit to members with appointments only. They got out of the car and headed in, Sofia following behind Katrina, who had been there countless times before.

"Yes," Katrina responded confidently to the woman standing behind the counter with an open bottle of wine in her hand. The winery was beautiful, with an outdoor tasting room that had an Italianesque feel to it: plenty of olive trees, lavender plants, and big rounds of hay that could be used for sitting or as a table. A cobbled path led to a sunflower patch, along with a few Adirondack chairs for sitting at the very end. And as they had hoped for, the fog layer had now burned off and the sun was shining as brightly as the flowers in the garden. After sampling several whites, followed by a few reds, Katrina selected a bottle and the two ambled along the path toward the Adirondacks, still chatting easily and enjoying one another's company. They continued to talk, and as they did, Katrina began to gently inquire about the demise of Sofia's marriage.

"I never thought I would ever get divorced," Sofia offered.

"Who does, really?" Katrina had responded. "I mean, people don't say, 'til death do us part' if they don't think it is going to last."

"Right," Sofia had agreed. "But I was going to be different. My parents' divorce was just so painful, I never wanted to do that to my own children," she said. "Nope. I felt so strongly about it, I didn't even want to bring children into the world unless I was prepared to stay with their father forever," she said.

Katrina wanted to know. "So what happened?" she asked.

Sofia lowered her head ever so slightly and looked up shyly at Katrina, a coy grin on her face, and said softly, "I met you."

Katrina couldn't control her laughter and laughed out loud while taking another sip of wine. In an effort to swallow despite her overwhelming laughter, a few bits sprayed out of her mouth as she quickly reached for her napkin. Her eyes began to water as she struggled to regain her composure.

"Ohhhhhhh, pleeeeease!" she said dramatically. "Gimme a break! If that is true, then how do you explain the fact that you were already divorced when you moved down here?"

"Well," Sofia returned the banter. "I was already divorced, but meeting you cemented my decision. Once I met you, I knew I had made the right decision."

Sofia then reached for her wine, and took a sip, never letting her gaze stray from Katrina's blue-green eyes, not even for a second. Fortunately, Sofia caught herself and realized she was, perhaps, laying it on just a bit thick. Perhaps she better tone it down.

"Anyway," she changed her tone and sat upright, trying to change the mood, "After years of being lied to, going through bankruptcy, and feeling alone most of the time, I'd had it. I tried to hang in there, I really did. I had tried to leave him 10 years before, but I just couldn't do it. I went out looking for apartments and everything. When I got there, in the apartment I mean, I just broke down and cried. I drove back to my house, well, his parents' house where we were living, absolutely sobbing. I wanted to leave at that time, but I just wasn't ready to give up on my marriage, you know? I stayed for 10 more years before I really left for good. It wasn't easy and it still isn't.

But sometimes, doing the right thing is not always the easy thing to do. You know?"

"So what happened next?"

"You know what happened next, Katrina. I moved down here, got a job, and met you."

"So, would you say, you 'lived happily ever after'?"

Sofia tried to take another sip of her wine and realized she had already finished the glass. She stuck her eye inside and looked around, hoping that maybe there was a leak in the bottom that would explain the missing contents. She shrugged and put the glass back down.

"Getting there," she nodded, still looking squarely at Katrina. "I think my new motto would have to be, 'better late than forever.'"

It was all going so well in a day that couldn't have been more perfect. And then, without warning, the worst thing that ever could have happened - happened:

Sofia stood up from her chair, walked over to Katrina's chair, and squeezed in so that she was barely sitting down next to Katrina without falling. Next, she grabbed Katrina's arm, and

Katrina couldn't tell if that was a reflex to keep from falling or if Sofia was intentionally holding on to her arm. Katrina could feel herself tense up, and her breath quickened. This was extremely unexpected and embarrassing! *What is she doing?* Katrina wondered. Katrina quickly surveyed the landscape to see who might be watching. She felt her face get hot and knew it was red from the heat. The conversation stopped. Katrina panicked. *This is so awkward! What is going on?*

Katrina did a quick inventory of the amount of wine they'd had. *How much had it been? Surely it wasn't that much, just a tasting and a few glasses... Okay, okay, hold on a second,* she thought. She had to get out of here before someone saw them sitting together, squeezed into a chair meant for one. *Now what?* Fortunately, Sofia broke the awkward silence first.

"Would you like me to go sit back in my own chair?" Sofia asked.

Before she knew it, Katrina had practically shouted it. An emphatic, direct, and automated,

"Yes!"

Without another word, Sofia stood up, as tears began to roll down her face. She walked over to where her own chair sat empty and fell into it, her crying becoming louder. Katrina reached for the open bottle of wine in desperation. She was desperate to finish it to calm her nerves and desperate to cut Sofia off. Clearly, she didn't need anymore. Katrina poured a generous glass for herself. She drank it down, and immediately poured another. She absolutely couldn't believe this was happening. Sofia began to wail.

"I am so sorry, I didn't mean any disrespect," she sobbed, "I just don't know...ohhhhh, I am going to get fired!" She continued carrying on, her nose now running along with the tears. "Maybe I am going through a midlife crisis! I just don't know anymore...please don't fire me, I am so sorry...I honestly don't know what I was thinking. I am not even a lesbian! I promise! I... I... I...don't even like women. I mean, I like women, but not like that. I am not sure what I was thinking..."

Katrina tried her best to console Sofia, but now what she really needed was time to think. She wondered if she should report this incident to human resources, or just see how things went.

Never mind, she thought. It didn't matter. Right now, she just needed to get out of here, to get Sofia home, and as quickly as possible. Perhaps this attention (or was it a come-on?) would have been better received if Katrina wasn't her boss, but under the circumstances, she kept telling herself, she simply couldn't allow it.

Chapter 26 - Sofia

Fortunately, it was still Sunday when Sofia woke up and remembered what had happened the day before...with her boss! *Ooooooohhhhhh!* With that thought, she rolled back over in bed, put her pillow over her head, and tried as hard as she could to block it all out and go back to sleep, hopefully for at least the next year. After several more minutes of tossing and turning she realized her head was spinning with the events of yesterday, and there was no way she was going to be able to return to sleep.

Oooooooooohhhhhhhhhhhhhhhh! She continued to moan as she lay in bed in mental anguish from her poor decision yesterday. Right now she was beyond embarrassed. She was mortified, anguished, dumbstruck...*what HAD I been thinking?* In addition to feeling so low and stupid, suddenly, a thought struck her that caused her to panic: *WHAT IF I GET FIRED? What would I do? Where would I go?* Her heart began to race and so did her mind. She needed to calm down.

And then she heard the "beep beep" of her phone, indicating a text message had come in. It was from Katrina. *Oh my god!* she screamed inside herself. *Was this it? Her termination notice? She wasn't even going to get the luxury of waiting until Monday to find out she'd lost her job?* Sofia held her phone away from her as far as she could and tried to half look at the text with one eye closed, fearing what it might say.

"Good morning, Sofia. Just making sure you are feeling alright. Oh, and just a reminder that you have that truancy meeting in the morning with the family of little Gibson. See you then!" Sofia continued to hold her breath. Slowly, she began to breathe again as she realized she hadn't been fired. It sounded like she still had her job. With this new shot of confidence, Sofia quickly typed her response back:

"Katrina, I am so sorry about yesterday. I want to let you know that I take full responsibility for what happened. You mean a lot to me and I didn't mean to disrespect you."

Sofia waited. Nothing. She looked at the time. Two minutes passed by with still no response. Then 10 minutes...then 15. Sofia felt herself getting hot, and reminded herself to keep breathing. Her pulse quickened and she began to feel beads of sweat on her cheeks and forehead.

Why wasn't she responding? She knew Kat was near her phone as she had just texted her about the truancy meeting. She tried another approach, related to work, to see if this would garner a response:

"Oh, and regarding the truancy meeting, thank you for the reminder. I will handle it." *Bing.* Within seconds of this text, Sofia already received a response back from Katrina.

"Sounds good. Have a good day."

How strange, Sofia thought. *She is obviously getting all my text messages, but she is ignoring the personal ones. All I can think of is that this means we no longer have a personal relationship. She is keeping it strictly professional. Well,* Sofia thought, with mixed emotions, *perhaps I still have my job for now, but I really liked Kat. Unfortunately, I am going to have to find a way to get over these feelings, before they even really had a chance to get started.* This made her really sad. And she was still worried, besides. She didn't know what Katrina was really thinking. Perhaps Katrina would be contacting human resources in the morning and she was still going to be fired. This thought still terrified her, and she dreaded the thought of having to go to work in the morning.

Around 1 p.m. Sofia finally rolled out of bed and decided to continue being lazy by pouring herself a large container of vodka with cranberry juice and ice, and headed to the beach outside her house. She hoped that lying in the sunshine would perform the miracle that she so desperately needed right now. That after absorbing the sunshine for a few hours she would miraculously see the situation in a renewed light and feel better. But just in case this didn't work the way she hoped it would, the cocktail she had made would give her temporary relief. *Shit!* Just as she was heading out of the door to walk a few yards down to the harbor, she caught a glimpse of Duke outside, sitting on his patio talking to someone on his cell. She froze in her tracks as she pondered what to do. She was in no way up to another confrontation today. She hadn't seen him since she dropped off the note at his house, telling him what a jerk he was. *How had things gone from being off to such a great start to this, in such a short time? So much for Balboa being my "happiest place on earth,"* she thought. This was beginning to feel more like a nightmare. She couldn't remember the last time she had felt so low.

Sofia stood there in her living room for a few more minutes, her drink in one hand and the beach towel in the other, debating her options. Right outside her door was Duke. *Nope, not going to happen,* she thought. She did an about-face and headed back to her bedroom. She lifted up the window, looked both ways to make sure no one would see her, and threw one leg over the sill. She was going to lay down in the sun. Next she brought her other leg up to the sill, and within a minute she was outside, out of D's sight. She took a long swallow out of her water bottle to calm her nerves and found her way down to stake her claim in the sand. She had no further aspirations for the day other than to relax. This day had already been rough enough.

Chapter 27 - Char

Char must have dozed off again because the next time she opened her eyes she could tell it was dark outside, and she could hear the hospital staff delivering dinner to the residents down the hall. *And where was Gus? Hadn't he been in here with me earlier? What the heck was going on anyway?*

At that moment she heard someone outside her hospital room, which she assumed was food service. Instead, in walked what appeared to be Dr. Dreamy, whose real name, according to his badge, was Dr. Kelley. "Hi," Char blushed. This guy looked familiar, she thought. *Where had I seen him before?*

Dr. Kelley smiled warmly at her and introduced himself. "You took quite a spill out there," he said, "How are you feeling?"

Char, who was acutely aware of Dr. Kelley's age, which couldn't have been much older than her, glanced down at her hospital gown to make sure she was decent. Assured that she was, she returned her gaze to the handsome doctor standing in front of her and said, "Uh, okay, I guess. What happened?"

"Well," Dr. Kelley paused, choosing his words carefully, "you and I had quite an introduction earlier today. You had been in quite a hurry, running from security I believe, when you crashed into me at the end of the hallway as you rounded the corner. Is there something that we should know? We have contacted law enforcement, and if you're some sort of fugitive or have a warrant or anything, it would be best if you just tell me now before law enforcement takes over." *Oh my god!* Char flushed with embarrassment. "No, no, no! Not even close!"

"Well, it certainly appeared as though you were running from our security officer in the front lobby," he offered.

"Oh, no, no, that isn't it at all," Char answered, "I wasn't running away from anything so much as I was running toward something. My dog, actually," she offered.

"So that is YOUR dog?" Dr. Dreamy, or rather, Dr. Kelley, responded. "There's a woman down the hall who claimed that the dog is HER dog. Maybe I do need to have law enforcement come down to settle this. Were you sneaking in drugs or something like that?"

"No, no, nothing like that, officer, I mean, doctor." Char felt as though she was being interrogated. "No, I can explain. First of all, I have never had a run-in with law enforcement, ever, except for the time back in college when I...well, never mind." She decided there was no need to share that story from her past. "You see, there really is a simple explanation as to what I was doing."

"Go on," Dr. Kelley offered with one eyebrow raised. "I'm listening..."

"So your patient, down the hall? Valerie Parker? She's my friend and I've been watching her dog for her since she's been in the hospital. And, well, as you can see, he's quite large, and uh, quite strong. And we had come down here to visit her outside the hospital when someone from inside was leaving. Just as the door slid open, BAM! Gus pulled loose from me and I lost my grip on the leash. The next thing I knew, he had disappeared as I was being held up by security at the main entrance. He was saying something or other about Covid and no visitors, and well, I thought if I just ran and could catch up to Gus, we would be back outside in no time. Unfortunately, by the looks of it, things didn't exactly go according to plan. I really am so sorry, I didn't mean to run into you or hurt you or anything. You aren't going to sue me or anything, are you?"

"Well," Dr. Kelley's eyes laughed as his mouth curled up into a sly grin, "not so far, I'm not, but I could change my mind if you or Gus don't decide to start taking it a little more easy on me. You see this bruise right here?" Dr. Kelley turned his head to the right so that Char could see his left cheekbone. It had an unusual bump on it and a bluish blackish bruise. Something shiny, like a salve or cream of some sort, was covering it and making the light in the room reflect off of it. "Usually, I'm the one in charge. That's why my name badge says 'doctor' on it. Today, I had to play the role of the patient in getting this cleaned up."

Char was beyond mortified. As if she didn't feel bad enough, it had to happen to a doctor no less, and one that she found particularly attractive. She instinctively snuck a quick peek at his ring finger on his left hand, wanting to know if he was otherwise accounted for. She didn't think he was, but one could never be too sure nowadays, particularly in settings like this where people used their hands in their line of work. Besides, what was she thinking? She was going to run him over, damage his face, and then ask for a date? Just the thought made her cringe with embarrassment; it was beyond improbable. Furthermore, he already thought she was some sort of homeless fugitive running from justice who just happened to wander into the hospital with her dog, probably looking for a clean bathroom or scrap of food somewhere. Not only that, need she remind herself? He was not only a doctor but a good-looking one besides. Char was sure he was already taken or was turning down many opportunities for romance multiple times per day.

"Hello? Hello..." He waved his hand in front of her, smiling. "Perhaps you don't know me well enough, but I was joking. Well, not about the bruise and getting knocked over, but about suing you. That was my attempt at humor."

"Huh? Oh, right." Char's thoughts about her fantasy date had been interrupted by none other than Dr. Dreamy himself. "Oh, yeah, I get it," she smiled meekly, trying to show that at least she had a quick sense of humor. "Okay," she said, "well, anyway, I really am sorry for what happened."

Dr. Kelley turned to leave and promised her he would be there the next day to see how she was faring. She still had a dull ache in the back of her head and neck from the fall. She was going to have to stay in the hospital at least overnight in order to be kept under observation. Whenever a head injury was involved, Dr. Kelley had explained, there was always the fear of a concussion.

Embarrassed or not, Char knew she wasn't going anywhere.

Chapter 28 - Duke

Duke knew he must have been maturing because for the first time that he could honestly remember, he actually felt bad for insulting a woman other than his mother. As he sat on his front patio, overlooking the harbor, he caught sight of Sofia, sunbathing in her usual red bikini down by the water. It was another gorgeous Balboa afternoon. The clang of the ballasts on the moored boats rang in the background as the breeze blew them from side to side, causing the seagulls to temporarily take flight until the ballasts became still once again. Then the gulls would settle back down on their same spot until something in the distance caught their attention and they flew off in a new direction, far on the other side of the island. And so the rhythmic back and forth movement of the boats, the gulls, and the ensuing sounds they created became a simple melody, making it easy for beachgoers to be lulled to sleep as they lay ashore.

Duke put on his sunglasses, took a swig of his beer, and lit his favorite Cuban cigar. He continued to stare surreptitiously in Sofia's direction while he mulled over this most recent predicament that he always seemed to find himself in. He wore his favorite straw hat down low on his forehead, partially to block the sun and partially so he wouldn't be caught looking at Sofia from afar, like some kind of crazed stalker. It was bad enough already that she was so angry with him, and he didn't want to give her anything else to add to her list of complaints about him. *Puff, puff, puff*...the smoke rings hung in the air above his mouth while he thought of a way out of this latest dilemma. *Strange,* he thought. He hadn't even seen her leave her house. He was pretty sure he would have seen her come out as the only entrance was through the patio to the front door.

"Hmph," he said to no one in particular and went back to reading his newspaper as he always did to collect some interesting headlines for tonight's show. He tried his best to focus but was having trouble as he kept glancing at the red bikini on the beach, which was precisely why he needed another beer. The beer would relax him, he told himself, and the more relaxed, the better the focus.

"Meow." Duke felt something soft rub up against his leg, and he looked down to see Bonkers there, rubbing and meowing as if he too was trying to distract Duke from the business at hand.

"What do you want, big boy?" Duke asked. Next, he put his newspaper and cigar down on the table, reached down to grab Bonkers from off the ground, and placed him in his lap. "What do you think, old boy?" he asked. "Hmmm? Do you know the ways of women, huh? Go over there and ask her, would ya?" Bonkers responded with a sleepy yawn and nestled deeper into Duke's lap, his warm dark fur feeling hot against his bare chest. He began to purr and the next thing he knew, even Bonkers was no longer listening. Duke would have to figure this out on his own.

Duke sat for a few more minutes, trying to decide his next move. He felt as though he was in a human game of chess, and that his next move was going to be critical. Move to the right, he'd lose his pawn. Move on the diagonal, he'd risk his queen. He definitely didn't want to risk losing his queen. The only problem now, he pondered, was deciding which was which. Time was ticking and he only had a few more seconds before he'd forfeit his turn. Finally, after considering his options, Duke decided to try to match her at her own game. He picked up his notepad and pen, and began to write:

"Dear Miss Sofia," it began. No, wait. "Dear Ms. Sofia," *No, not that either,* he debated. Finally, due to utter exasperation and running out of other options, he decided to go the casual route:

"Sofia -

I got your note. I apologize if I insulted you. I am a radio talk show host and what I do best is say outrageous things to get good ratings. I realize now that what I did was objectify you and that was wrong. I hope you can forgive me. Sincerely, Duke."

With that, Duke took a long drag from his cigar and finished off his beer. He threw the empty bottle toward the can sitting next to the front door and missed. The noise of the can landing on the concrete patio frightened Bonkers, who abruptly ended his nap and hopped off Duke in search of a better place to catch some rays. Now freed of his cat that had been staking a claim on his lap, Duke stood up and walked across the patio, opened the picket fence gate, and walked up to Sofia's door. He checked the handle, locked. He looked around and saw a small pot of red geraniums to the left of the door, which he moved closer and slipped his note under it where it could be seen. Sofia would have to notice it in order to get inside her house. Feeling unusually sheepish and not wanting to face a confrontation, Duke then walked back to his house and slipped inside without being seen. He was almost safe inside when he heard clawing at the front door and returned to open it. "So much for handling the Sofia situation for me, you damn cat," Duke said. Without wasting another second, Duke let Bonkers slip inside the house and closed the door. There was nothing to do now but wait.

Chapter 29 - Valerie

Three hours later, Valerie woke and noticed it was dark beyond the window in her hospital room. She must have slept the afternoon away, and she stumbled around in her brain as she tried to bring to light the events that had occurred earlier that afternoon. She was trying to decipher what had been real and what had been part of her Xanax-induced dream. She looked to the side of the bed and noticed Gus sleeping on the floor, with his leash tied to her bed. "Oh, right..." She frowned and looked back toward the window, trying to deny the reality of the situation, but couldn't. Her dog was, very much, in fact, with her. This meant there was no denying the truth about what had happened, as well as the events that had led to the request for additional Xanax.

On the positive side, she was starting to feel a tad better and wondered when she might be leaving the hospital. She decided she would ask her doctor later that day. In the meantime, she needed to talk to Char. She still had no idea how Gus had wound up in her hospital room. She also wondered about Char—*where was she?* She had tried asking her nurse about her friend but was only told something about HIPAA violations and looked apologetically at Valerie despite not giving her the answer she so desperately wanted right now. *What was that supposed to mean?* she wondered. The last time she checked, HIPAA laws only applied to the patients, but whatever. Frustrated, she dismissed her irritation with the nurse. With her right arm, she reached over the side of the bed and gave Gus a scratch on the head. He responded to this with a sloppy lick and went back to sleep on the cold ceramic floor. Valerie reached around for her phone and picked it up. She texted Char and waited. Nothing. Restless and confused, she tried to entertain herself by surfing the web, but all she saw was more tiresome discourse about the Covid pandemic and the impending election. She was tired of hearing about both. She put down her phone and picked up the TV remote. Perhaps there would be something there that would capture her interest. *Here we go,* she thought, *I'll just settle for watching old sitcom reruns.* Something light that would make her laugh. As she found herself settling in and beginning to become lost in the current episode, she looked up and couldn't believe her eyes. Her nurse, Ellen, was back. But instead of bringing in dinner as she had expected based on it being past 5:30

p.m., Ellen brought in a gurney with none other than Char in the bed! Valerie could not believe her eyes! *What in the world had happened?*

She still felt the lingering effects of the Xanax, and couldn't help but wonder if this was all really happening. She was so stunned that words escaped her, and she kept looking back and forth between Gus, who was now up off the floor and wagging his tail feverishly, and Char, trying to make sense of everything.

Nurse Ellen was the first to speak. "HIPAA laws prevent me from disclosing patient information, but if I need to double up your room by bringing in another patient, well, I still haven't told you who the patient is now, have I?" With that, Nurse Ellen, who thankfully was slim enough to squeeze in between the two beds which were now crowded in the room, reached behind Valerie's bed and pushed it closer to the wall, making just enough space to squeeze Char in her bed next to Valerie's. Both girls smiled at one another as they couldn't believe how funny this was.

"Char, what happened? Are you okay? I am so sorry..." But before she could ask the 50 more questions that were circling inside her head, Char deliberately cut her off, wanting to reassure her.

"Don't worry!" she said, "I will be just fine. Please don't be mad at Gus, this really isn't his fault. He is just a dog, and, well..." She changed her thoughts mid-sentence. "Did you know he is real, I mean really, strong?" Char then explained the entire sordid affair to Valerie, including how she had chased Gus down the hallway and had bumped into Dr. Kelley, aka Dr. Dreamy, and had fallen and hit her head. "Really, I'm fine," she continued. "They just want to keep me here for observation. You know...the head thing. Doctors get super nutted up anytime there's head trauma.

I suspect they're also keeping me here in case there is a warrant out for my arrest," she laughed. Char explained everything from the beginning, leading up to the false allegations that she had been homeless and was a fugitive from the law. They both laughed.

When they finally stopped laughing, Valerie became serious. "Thank you," she said.

"For what?" Char countered. "For getting us both possibly sued and winding up with legal matters? Uh, not following here, Val."

"For being such a terrific friend, Char. I love you. Look at everything you've done for me. And I was getting super lonely here, all by myself. They won't let visitors into the hospital, and now look! You figured out a way to not just get in the door, but to be able to stay in my room here with me, and with Gus, too! Who does that? Knowing you, you probably had this entire thing planned from the beginning. But even if you didn't," she paused, wiping a stray tear from her cheek, "thank you. I am glad to know there is still some good in this world."

With that, Char reached out across the two beds and grabbed her friend's hand. "Yes," she said, "you are right. There is still good in the world. A lot of it." Char continued her gaze on Valerie, thinking what a dark place Val must be in. She didn't normally talk like this. Then again, there wasn't much that was "normal" going on in the world at this moment, period. Char suddenly felt the need to lighten the mood. "Besides, do you know who I bumped into?" she asked as a sly smile spread across her face. "Dr. Kelley, otherwise known to me as Dr. Dreamy. I can't help but wonder if he's single."

As she had hoped, this statement had returned the smile to Val's face. "Oh Char," she mused, "you, my friend, are incorrigible!" The two friends smiled. One was happy for the renewed companionship, the other content to be able to comfort her friend. But perhaps the happiest one of all in the room that day was Gus, who had managed to hop up on the two beds, a better part of himself squarely positioned on each.

Chapter 30 - Katrina

As Katrina drove into work Monday morning it was with mixed emotions. The professional side of her was battling with her emotional side. She knew which side she wanted to win, but what would the cost be? After arriving at the office, she decided to go about her day much in the usual way, as she honestly didn't know what else to do. She wasn't mad or upset, rather, simply conflicted. And because she really did like Sofia, she didn't want to go to HR or be vindictive. She hoped they could return to business as normal, maybe just forget it ever happened? She decided that Sofia was probably hurting more than she was, and so decided to be the one to take the initiative to clear the air. As soon as her first meeting was over this morning, she would walk across the street to see Sofia, just to sort of check in, so to speak, and see how she was doing. It was around 9:30 when she stepped out of her meeting, took a big cleansing breath, and worked up the nerve to do what she knew she wanted to do. She walked across the street and over to Harbor Street

Elementary. "Morning, Katrina. Sofia's back in her office," the secretary greeted her warmly. "Shall I let her know you are here? Is she expecting you?"

"That's all right," Katrina smiled back. "You are busy," she said as she continued walking.

"I will see myself in." Sofia's door was slightly ajar and so Katrina gave it a gentle knock before pushing it open and walking in. Sofia had her back to Katrina as she was sitting at her desk, and Katrina thought she noticed the ever-so-slight straightening of her back and stiffening of her long neck as she entered the office. Without turning around, Sofia continued typing and responded in a customary manner back. There were no pleasantries, no eye contact, nothing but cold and hurtful professionalism. The forced politeness and lack of any genuine emotion forced Katrina to realize how much she too was hurting. It felt terrible looking at Sofia, her back still facing her, knowing she was embarrassed and humiliated. As Katrina stood there gazing at Sofia, all she could think about was how much she wanted to comfort her and hug her.

Instead, she was forced to stand there cold and awkward, keeping her distance and thinking about how much she actually admired Sofia.

Much of Katrina's success was due to the fact that Katrina always kept her emotions in check, especially her strong ones. As much as it had caused her discomfort, Katrina admired how Sofia had been willing to put herself out there, staying true to her own thoughts and feelings and willing to take a risk. While it may not have been the smartest risk she could have taken, there was still something to be said for having the courage and bravery to lay it all on the line. Katrina continued to struggle inside herself. But her position, her title, and her career had taken years to build. She was not going to lay that all on the line, no matter what she felt about Sofia. So instead of telling her what she was thinking, Katrina did what she always did, which was to play it smart. She continued with her poker face and tried to think of something nonchalant and casual to discuss.

"Pretty nice weather today, don't you think?" she tried. Surely Sofia would be able to see she was making an effort, without crossing any lines or bringing up the weekend. Katrina tried desperately a few more times with idle conversation, bringing up the Lakers, the recent Covid statistics, etc. until there was nothing more she could think of to say. She turned to leave when Sofia, suddenly and abruptly, spun around in her chair to face Katrina.

"Katrina," she said. "I really want to apologize. I hope you can forgive me. I promise, nothing like that will ever happen again, ever. I mean it. I am so genuinely sorry."

Even under the stress and the lines around her eyes, Katrina still thought Sofia was cute.

She couldn't help it. But again, she reminded herself, *Poker face! Remain stoic! Don't let her see your emotions!*

And then, because she couldn't help herself, Sofia became brutally honest. "The worst part of all," she lamented, "is that now you're not going to want to hang out with me anymore, and I've lost the one friend I had down here. But it's okay," she said, "I get it."

What came next was a surprise that Sofia certainly didn't see coming, not for a million years. Instead of agreeing that the two of them would never ever spend time together outside of work ever again, Katrina laid down a verbal curveball that was completely unexpected. "No, that's not necessarily true," she said kindly. "I actually do need to go to another winery this weekend and pick up another shipment since they are all being delivered right now. You are welcome to join me if you want."

Huh? What? Sofia couldn't believe her ears. *What is happening right now? This was absolutely crazy; it made absolutely no sense.* Sofia looked to the right, then to the left. She didn't know what she was looking for except for answers that weren't hiding in the room. This wasn't an episode of *Candid Camera*, and there was no one else in the room to ask, "Did I hear this right?"

So even though she didn't understand it, she found herself nodding in agreement. "Yes, absolutely," she said after she'd recovered. And with that, she quickly swung her chair back around so as not to be seen, and began typing feverishly at her desk. She waited for Kat to leave before she completely collapsed on her desk, no longer feeling as though she had to pretend to be working. She remained frozen for a few minutes, trying to recover and make sense of what had just happened. As many times as she replayed every detail around in her head, it just didn't add up.

Like any good unlicensed internet attorney, she replayed the facts over and over in her head:

1. She had hit on her boss.
2. Her boss had denied her.
3. They are now going out again this weekend.

What was she missing? In her own life, Sofia knew that there was no way she would ever spend time with someone that she knew had a love interest in her if she didn't feel the same way, as that would be incredibly uncomfortable. So why then was Katrina willing to spend time with her, especially knowing how Sofia felt about her? It made no sense. Surely Katrina had better things to do than to spend more time with someone who she knew had an unrequited love interest in her, unless she just felt sorry for her? Regardless, Sofia thought about how seldom we get a second chance in life. This was her second chance (which, by the way, further endeared her to Katrina). She was not going to blow it, she promised herself. No, she knew how horrible she had felt before. She knew how close she'd come to almost losing her job. This was her one last opportunity to put the mistake she made last weekend where it belonged, in the past. She looked forward to proving to Katrina that she would honor this gift of a second chance and that they could be friends.

Sofia slowly tried to return her focus to work but found herself stewing more. These feelings she had for Katrina, what were they, anyway? She had never been drawn to a woman, ever. Perhaps it was a momentary fleeting thing, as she had heard all her life that people were born gay or they weren't. Sofia was definitely not born gay since she was nearing 50 and had never kissed a woman before, never thought about a woman in that way before, ever. Logically, intellectually, it just didn't make sense. All of her conditioning, social constructs, beliefs, education, and life experiences had never called into question that she was, in fact, straight. Until now. But why? It was precisely this inner knowing, this inner feeling, that made these thoughts feel spiritual. They went against the law of the land. They went against man's law. Perhaps that's why the only explanation for them was that they came from some other place. The only other place that Sofia felt deep inside her was a connection to the heavens and the spiritual world through her connection to the earth and to nature. She couldn't pinpoint it exactly, no. But she also couldn't think of any other place these feelings could have come from. And although they would have to remain locked away inside her, there was a part of her that still didn't believe that Katrina didn't feel them too.

Chapter 31 - Sofia

The rest of the workweek left Sofia feeling slightly better than how she had felt in the beginning. It was now springtime on the island, which meant there was more daylight to enjoy after work, despite Covid. In order to deal with the stress of work, plus the recent events with Kat and Duke as well, Sofia had begun dealing with her weight (which had recently been creeping up), and her other problems, by taking brisk walks around the island in the evenings to sort through her thoughts and emotions that she didn't have time to sort through during the workday. Not only did she enjoy the salty sea breeze that filled her lungs, but the sights from the beautiful potted flowers along the walkways and patios were so very pretty. It was one of the reasons she loved it here, as everyone seemed to take pride in their houses and the weather was just perfect for growing these beautiful plants. As she walked along the boardwalk, she thought about everything going on in her life and tried to focus on the positive. She was undoubtedly happy that she had successfully transitioned her life to the place of her childhood dreams and landed a great job that would enable her to stay here and enjoy it for as long as she wanted. And although she had been incredibly embarrassed by last weekend's unforeseen (or were they foreseen, if she was being honest?) circumstances, she was relieved that no real harm had come from it and that she and Katrina now seemed to be getting back on track. And as far as her irritating neighbor Duke, she was even starting to soften towards him as well.

On the one hand, he had been a complete jerk, nearly jeopardizing her reputation simply by the fact that he advertised, on the radio, that she had been hanging out with him. He was not good for her reputation, as he was smug, offensive, and crass. Sharing the fact that they had hung out together was damaging to her reputation, and he ought to have considered that before he broadcast their dinner details all over Orange County.

On the other hand, she wasn't one to talk. She had nearly damaged her own reputation by her own actions with her boss at work. Fortunately, it was now appearing as though Kat was going to take the high ground and be tight-lipped about it. Furthermore, since she certainly was capable of making mistakes, and had been forgiven, didn't it then make sense to forgive Duke for his mistake as well? Although she really didn't appreciate being spoken about in those sexualized terms (well, okay, it was sort of flattering for a woman of her age), at least he had apologized. *Yes*, she thought, *Duke had apologized to me, just as I had apologized to Kat. Perhaps I ought to extend the same courtesy to Duke as had been extended to me?* she thought.

She continued to circle around the island at the same pace. Similarly, her mind continued its loop from work, to Kat, to Duke, and back again. As long as she circled, so did her mind. By the time she was done, she was too tired from both walking and thinking to do much of either anymore. And so this became Sofia's form of self-care. *Much healthier than drinking a bottle of wine each evening,* she thought.

Sofia had finished her last circle around the island and had just turned left onto her street when she suddenly stopped short. There he was: Duke. It was one thing to think things over in her head, but another to figure out what to say to him. That was supposed to be tomorrow night's musings, and she wasn't prepared to actually speak real words out loud to him this evening. How dare he! Didn't he know she was still in her pondering phase and needed time to think through how she really felt first so that she would know what to say when she finally did see him?

So there she stood, frozen, on the sidewalk, two doors down from her house. Conversely, Duke stood still where he was, watching Sofia. It was a virtual standoff with rules of engagement that neither one knew, and no one had remembered wanting to play. But here they were, and Sofia felt the pressure to move first, as she realized she looked quite awkward and unusual coming to a complete stop in the road just two doors down from her house. *Quick!* she pressured herself. *Think of something! You look ridiculous! Say something to play this off or you are about to lose face!* Quickly, she felt around her pockets and took her keys out dramatically in hopes that Duke would think she had stopped to gather them before reaching her house. "Here they are!" she said, hoping she was loud enough that he would hear her. She then took one deliberate step in front of the other, trying to figure out what she was going to say next. She thought briefly about falling to the ground and faking an epileptic attack in order to avoid the ensuing confrontation and then realized that she probably should rehearse that beforehand. She was left with no choice except to keep walking and get this over with.

Fortunately, he broke the ice before she did, which relieved her of having to come up with something to say. "My cat wrote you a letter," he shouted. "Did you get it?"

Sofia couldn't help but crack a smile. "Um, I did receive a letter, it was under my geraniums by my door, but I didn't realize it was from your cat," Sofia replied. "Particularly because it said 'Sincerely, Duke' at the end," Sofia laughed at her own joke.

"Right, right," Duke replied with a straight face. "That's because my cat is always messing things up for me, and then trying to fix it. He is too ashamed to just come out and admit it, so he blames me. Hence, he wrote my name at the bottom." Duke grinned and pointed towards Bonkers, who was currently sleeping on the patio absorbing the last patch of sunlight before the sun retired completely for the day. "In fact, he looks really innocent over there, but really, he's the cause of all my troubles," he continued.

"Really?" Sofia asked with an incredulous look on her face. "That's really interesting, I must have had it completely backwards," she said. "And to think, this whole time I thought it was you who had said all of those crass things about me on the radio. You are lucky I didn't get a restraining order against you. Perhaps you can give me the phone number of your cat's probation officer or something." Sofia felt her mood lightening. Perhaps her evening walk around the island really had done her some good. Or perhaps it was just this island that continued to have this soothing effect on her. It was, after all, the reason she had always referred to it as her happiest place on earth; it always had been, and she knew it always would be.

"Okay, okay," Duke reached towards her. "You got me. It was me. I apologize. Do you forgive me?"

Sofia decided she wasn't quite ready to give up the banter after all, "Wait, Duke. Hold on a sec. What are you saying? Are you saying your cat, Bonkers, really isn't attracted to me? Do you mean it was you all along? I am so hurt by your deception. And here I was so flattered! No member of the feline family has ever come on to me before. And Bonkers, well, he is just so paws-itively..." Unable to contain herself any further, she burst out laughing. "You know what Duke? At first, when I heard how you spoke about me on the radio, I was really...pissed. But then, I thought about it. And I realized we all make mistakes.

Unfortunately, I've made a few of my own this past week, and, so yeah. Let's just move on. Tell Bonkers that I accept his apology."

Duke grinned that award-winning grin of his and Sofia thought it really was a waste that he wasn't on camera where people could see him. He was really good-looking. And handsome. And good looking, and... Her thoughts were suddenly interrupted.

"So that's it? We're friends again?"

"Well," she smiled, "I wouldn't exactly go that far, but you can let Bonkers know that I do have one small request that might help move things in that direction."

"Sure," Duke played along. "What shall I tell Bonkers?"

"I've always wanted to learn to surf," Sofia said. "My dad taught me to body surf here at Corona del Mar when I was a kid, but I want to learn how to surf on a surfboard. Do you think
Bonkers would be able to set up some lessons for me?"

"I'll ask," Duke responded. "He's a little busy sleeping right now, as you can see. And he isn't likely to be helpful if I wake him up and interrupt his sleep. But I'll ask him if he knows anyone who could help you out once he wakes up."

"Thanks," Sofia responded, this time with a genuine smile. "Have a nice night." "You too," he answered.

They both turned and waved and went into their respective houses, satisfied with the turn of events. Sofia in particular had an added lightness about her. She was looking forward to her prospective surf lessons and tomorrow would be Saturday, time to spend with Kat.

Chapter 32 - Char

"This is the best hospital stay ever!" Valerie said enthusiastically to Char, who still had not been released from the hospital yet due to the swelling on her head.

"Okay, okay, I am glad you are doing better," Char replied. "It's not exactly like this is Club Med or anything... I hate to be a downer, but we're here for a reason, you know. No one gets to hang out in the hospital unless there's something wrong," Char reminded her upbeat friend."

"That's not true," Valerie quipped back. "Just look at Gus over there. He's here, and he doesn't have anything wrong with him," she countered.

"You have a point there, my friend, he is here, for now. But I am sure they aren't going to let him stay here."

"Well, we certainly can't take him," Valerie shot back, "because we're still here!" And with that, Valerie continued to paint her nails a pretty pink while watching a romantic comedy on TV, all the while catching up on the latest gossip with Char and stopping only occasionally to pet Gus. For Valerie, her hospital stay had just improved 110 percent, as she had gone from being all alone with nothing but the current events and the pandemic to consider, not to mention how she was going to make money once she got out of there. With her friend and best canine companion there, suddenly things had taken a major upturn. Besides that, Valerie delighted in trying to play matchmaker between Char and the doctor (Dr. Kelley, was it?) she had bumped into. Although Char thought the chances of an intentional meeting (as opposed to the one that had occurred in the hallway unintentionally and had left them both injured) were slim to none, she didn't mind talking to Valerie about it because it was fun and gave them both something positive to focus on for a while. *Anything to keep Val's spirits up,* she thought.

The two girls were just finishing up their evening meal brought in by the hospital staff when Dr. Kelley was making his rounds and walked in. The bruise on his left cheek had now changed colors from purple and red to more of a green and yellow, but overall the swelling had gone down. Even with the bruise, Valerie agreed that he was definitely a handsome guy. He walked in with his clipboard and took a look to review his notes before stopping to speak to them.

"Homeless fugitive with dog," his notes reminded him.

"Oh yes," he said as he looked at both of them and went back to his notes. Now that they were both in hospital gowns with Gus laying in between the two of them, he couldn't remember offhand who was who. He knew the one who had run into him in the hallway was being monitored for a concussion, while the other was in for pancreatitis. The dog, he wondered, well, he didn't know what he was still doing here. He made a mental note to himself to inquire about that with the nurses after he left the room. *Perhaps he has nowhere to go,* he thought to himself. *But still, last time I checked, this was a hospital, not some sort of therapy wing where we have these kinds of things...* Although Dr. Kelley was in fact single, he also had his standards to uphold and made it a policy to never date his patients. The dog, however, was not part of the policy, and Dr. Kelley did have a soft spot for the poor...what was he anyway? Some sort of pit bull? Mutt? Anyway, he did have a soft spot for the dog, who hadn't bit or bothered anyone, despite the rumors. Although the girls were off-limits, the dog was not. And he offered to both girls (since he still wasn't sure who the rightful owner really was) to take Gus home until they got out of the hospital to care for him themselves.

Valerie, who was already on top of the world due to the recent turn of events, now raised the volume of her voice five more decibels in an equal combination of astonishment and delight.

"Really? Are you serious? OMG, doctor! Thank you so much! I absolutely can't believe this! This hospital is the best ever! Can I come back here next time? I mean, well, I know it isn't exactly a hotel or anything, but boy, it sure feels nice here!" Dr. Kelley chuckled as he made his way out of the room.

"Dr. Kelley," Char called after him, "When do you think we will be able to leave?

"Tomorrow morning for the one who ran into me, Char, if you still feel well in the morning. We just want to make sure that there is no additional swelling in your brain and that you didn't suffer a major concussion. If you feel fine in the morning, you will be free to go. As for Valerie, I am sorry. Although I know you're starting to feel better, I think a lot of it is having your friend here, and Gus too, I'm afraid. I'm going to need you to stay at least a few more days until your blood panels get better and you can feel this well without your pain medication. As far as Gus goes, well, he appears to have a perfect bill of health, and is welcome to leave this evening with me, after my shift is over."

"Thank you, doctor," Char gushed in spite of herself. At this point, she honestly wasn't sure if she wanted to be released from the hospital or not. The longer she stayed, she reasoned, the more time she would have to work her magic with Dr. Dreamy and hopefully be able to line up a date. *Not that a handsome doctor hasn't had opportunities like that before,* she reminded herself. *But still, it doesn't hurt to try.* And right now, she had nothing to lose other than his already poor image of her as a homeless fugitive running from the law. That was one image she was certainly willing to shed.

Although Valerie was disappointed to hear that she would still have to stay while Char and Gus would most likely get to go home sooner rather than later, she couldn't have agreed with Dr. Kelley more. She always knew the importance that a great attitude and positivity play in healing, and was disappointed in herself that she had allowed herself to become so negative earlier. It made sense that now that her friend was here, keeping her mind off of things and finding things to laugh about, she had begun to feel better. She needed to remember to do this even after Char and Gus went home if she wanted to be strong and on her own again soon. The events of yesterday and today had definitely driven home this point.

Both Valerie and Char had had a fantastic day just being together, despite having been in the hospital. They used up a lot of energy laughing and talking, and it wasn't long after dinner that the orderly had come by and turned out the lights in their room so that the only lights that remained were the glow of the television and the light emanating from the hallway. By the time Dr. Kelley got off work and came by to take Gus home for a few days, neither girl was awake. He wrote them a quick note and taped it on the wall behind their beds, where one of them would be sure to see it in the morning. Having done that, he unleashed Gus, who was happy to be untied and led him down to his car. Fortunately, Dr. Kelley had a convertible, as Gus took up most of the front seat. Never forgetting he was a doctor and that patient health and safety always came first, Dr. Kelley stretched the seatbelt in the front passenger's seat around Gus and buckled him in safely. Gus seemed to intuit that he was in good hands and made no effort to escape. As Dr. Kelley drove down Pacific Coast Highway, Gus rode quietly alongside. The two were both content as they left the hospital and headed up to Dr. Kelley's beautiful house in Newport Beach, with the warm air all around. Having just officially met, Gus and Dr. Kelley appeared to all who passed them on the road as though they were the best of friends.

Chapter 33 - Katrina

Katrina dressed in her favorite Hawaiian shirt and a pair of shorts and slid her feet into her newest pair of Cole Haan sandals before heading out the door to pick up Sofia. She tried not to think too deeply about anything, particularly last weekend, as this would only complicate matters.

Despite having been genuinely flattered by Sofia's advances, she had set the record straight and was looking forward to a drama-free day. Katrina considered herself a bit of a wine connoisseur and was happy to have some company as she headed once again toward Temecula to pick up another wine shipment. Although she could have had her wines shipped to her house, Katrina preferred to make a day of it, an excuse to hop into her convertible and go for a long drive with the top down to a beautiful locale. Once there, she would enjoy a glass or two of her favorite wine before heading back, usually in time to watch the sunset over the Pacific Ocean. It wasn't exactly a hobby per se, more like a pastime. It was something she really looked forward to each weekend after her long work week. As she rounded the corner she caught sight of Sofia, already out front on her patio, watering her flowers and exchanging pleasantries with Duke. This was a stark contrast from the week before when Sofia and Katrina had joked about running over his surfboard with her car. Curious, she would have to ask Sofia what had happened between the two of them, now that they were clearly back to being on speaking terms again.

The drive into Temecula was cool and relaxed. The duo found easy conversation despite the extra noise of the wind coming in over the top of the convertible. Although friendly and talkative, Katrina noticed a subtle difference in Sofia. Perhaps her body language was slightly more closed, her language a tad more reserved, almost imperceivable but a change that Kat detected nonetheless. It was understandable considering what had happened last weekend. This would be the chance for both women to erase the mishap from their friendship and move forward.

As the two checked out with their bottles of wine, it was getting close to lunch and Katrina suggested a restaurant right around the corner that she had been to before. It was inside an old bank building and had a beautiful bar inside as well as big tall booths for dining. Sofia and Katrina had to wait for a good 20 minutes before their table would be ready, so they sat at the tall bar and ordered a drink while they waited. It wasn't long before they were called to their table, so they settled up with the bartender and followed the waitress to their table.

Katrina and Sofia continued talking and shared their favorite music playlists. Katrina noted how similar their taste in music was. The connection the two shared was palpable and rare, and Katrina knew it. As Katrina sat eating her lunch, her mind kept drifting to romance with Sofia. As much as she tried to fight it, the feeling she had growing inside her was something she couldn't, or chose not to, ignore. She realized the risk she would be taking by succumbing to her feelings, but sitting there at the table across from Sofia, she suddenly decided it was a risk she wanted to take. She had always made the smart choice, and for once, she was going to make a decision that perhaps wasn't the most intelligent one, but one that had the potential to make her incredibly happy. She knew that from this moment on if Sofia was still willing, she would be open to exploring her feelings for Sofia. And that is where the real magic began.

As Katrina sat on her side of the table, knowing there was a shift, knowing suddenly that she wasn't willing to let her potential for happiness pass her by due to some job, it happened. Caught up in the moment, the details and exact words fell on deaf ears, but she somehow had understood what Sofia was asking her. She nodded in the affirmative and glanced down at her plate to take another bite when she felt the kiss on her cheek, just as she had before. This time, she knew she was receptive to Sofia's affections, and waited, with her heart pounding, for Sofia to return to the table from the ladies' room.

No more needed to be said because they both understood what was happening. And as they left the restaurant, Sofia took the lead and held on to Katrina's arm. They continued to walk around the shops of the quaint little town, arm in arm, stopping only to go into Katrina's favorite cheese shop for some samples. Once outside the store they found each other's arms once again and continued in this manner back to the car.

Once inside the car, it was Sofia who spoke first. "I was not going to do this today," she said. "I absolutely wasn't going to do this. You gave me a second chance, and you're my boss, and I wanted to not blow my second chance because how often do people get a second chance and I don't even know what happened but you said or did something that let me know it was okay. It is okay, isn't it?"

Sofia had been talking so fast and had spoken so many words that Katrina feared she was going to hyperventilate. Katrina reached for Sofia's hand and held it gently as she said, "Breathe,

Sofia. And yes, it is okay." Katrina then leaned in and laid a gentle and warm kiss on Sofia's lips. The kiss was soft and tender, and Katrina could feel Sofia relax as she pulled away and looked lovingly into Sofia's eyes.

"But, but, but...I don't understand," Sofia said, "I, I, I thought that with your job and everything..."

"You're right," Katrina agreed. "But then I thought about it, and I reconsidered. It is definitely a risk, so we will have to be extremely careful, but, well, I'm willing to give it a try."

Katrina turned on the engine, this time leaving the roof of the convertible up as it was close to dusk and cooling off. As they headed home, they held hands and Sofia leaned up against Katrina's side since she was driving. They were quiet and content while still a little nervous. They were embarking on uncharted territory, which was a gamble, particularly at work. It was a risk, Katrina knew, but one she had decided that she was willing to take.

Chapter 34 - Char

It was with mixed emotions that Char left the hospital early Monday morning. She was excited to be going home but realized it was less and less likely that she would be able to see Dr. Kelley anymore, let alone convince him to go out with her. At least she had an excuse to see him one last time, she thought, as she would need to go get Gus and bring him home. It would be at least another week or more before Val would be discharged, and the thought of leaving her friend in the hospital by herself plagued her with guilt. However, Char really tried to run her life by analyzing what was and what wasn't in her control, and she knew that Valerie being stuck in the hospital was definitely not anything that Char had control over. What she could do, however, was go get Gus, and take good care of him. Which reminded her that she probably ought to start taking good care of herself as well. It had been months since she had worked out other than the few runs around the island with Gus. Since Val had gotten sick, she had been unable to continue their workouts. But Char knew that she was able to take responsibility for her health anyway, and needed to get back on track. This she had control over.

As Char arrived back home and was putting on some clean clothes, she remembered to pull Dr. Kelley's note out of her pants pocket to see about contacting him about bringing Gus home. However, that would have to wait. Within 15 minutes she was headed out the door and on her way to the gym. At least she didn't have to feel guilty for leaving Gus behind.

She dialed the number on the note and waited for Dr. Kelley to answer. He didn't, so she left a voicemail, trying to sound casual and not let her voice betray her nervousness. "Hi Dr. Kelley," she said smoothly, " It's Char, eh...from the hospital. You probably already know this, but uh, I am home now. So yeah. ...I can come to get Gus anytime. Bye!"

Ok...not so smooth, she thought. She was so nervous, she even forgot to leave her number.

Oh my god! she thought. *Now I'm going to have to call him back, and he's going to think I'm stalking him.* She decided to wait a while so as to not appear overly stalker-like.

Now that she was back home, Char changed her mind about going to the gym as she realized that what she wanted instead, more than anything at this moment was a nice hot shower in her own house. In her rush to get something clean on, Char had forgotten about a fresh shower.

Now that she had her clean clothes on but still smelled like the hospital, it wasn't the same. She immediately took off her clean clothes, threw those in the dirty pile, and decided to start again with a hot shower and fresh, clean clothes. It felt so good to be home and in her own space! And she was no worse for wear after her unfortunate fall, although she did concede privately that she may have made some different choices if she had a do-over. *Oh well,* she thought. *Perhaps some good came from it after all,* she said to herself as she pictured Dr. Dreamy, Gus, and how happy Valerie had been. In hindsight, a small bump on the head had turned out to be a small price to pay.

She had just finished putting the last touches of her makeup on and felt like her old self again when her doorbell rang. Surprised, Char froze for a minute, thinking, *Now who could this be? Fortunately, I'm decent,* she thought. Twenty minutes earlier and she wouldn't have been. *Perhaps it was some delivery guy, FedEx, or something,* she thought as she walked to the door. "Coming!" she called out as she made her way to the front door. She swung the door open and standing there in front of her, leash in hand, was none other than Dr. Kelley, aka Dr. Dreamy, himself! "Wow! Hi! Oh my goodness!" she said, clearly caught off guard. She glanced down at the other end of the leash and there lay Gus, looking hot and tired on this rare 90-degree day on Balboa. "So, how is he? How did you find my house? Do you want to come in?" she asked all at once. Dr. Kelley laughed and looked down at his watch. He was dressed in street clothes, something Char had never seen him in, and said, "Actually, if you don't mind, I think both Gus and I could really use a glass of water."

Char couldn't believe what was happening! Here was Dr. Dreamy, in flesh and blood, in her living room! She had never expected this turn of events in a million years! She tried not to notice, but she couldn't help it. His white lab coat and stethoscope hadn't done him justice compared to his jeans and t-shirt. He was all southern California-esque, and Char liked that he didn't seem to flaunt that he was a doctor when he was off duty. In fact, he had on flip-flops which showed that he clearly spent far too much time at work because his feet were stark white! *Still, that was oh so minor,* Char thought. Her thoughts then turned to her own appearance, and for once, Char was delighted that she had just spent all that time gussying herself up after having felt so grungy the past few days. More than anything she wanted to impress Dr. Kelley, and they hadn't exactly gotten off to the best start at the hospital. "Pretty nice place for a homeless person," he quipped, looking around and admiring the view. They both laughed.

"Yes, well," she countered, as she handed him his water and poured some into a dish for Gus. "You wouldn't believe me, but I told you I wasn't exactly homeless," she said. "What about you? Where do you call home?" She asked as she flashed him her biggest and flirtiest smile.

Dr. Kelley guzzled down his water and placed it back on the kitchen counter before responding. "I can't tell you that," he lied. "I have living proof that you aren't actually homeless, as I looked up your address at work. But how do I know that you really aren't a stalker? I mean, the way you flew at me past the security guard, we haven't had that happen since pre-Covid."

Char could tell by the way he was smiling at her that he wasn't serious but was still continuing with this part of the initial joke back at the hospital. She also took the opportunity to look up close at his face once more, and noticed the bruise was even less noticeable than it had been just yesterday. Feeling awkward and not knowing what to say, she changed the subject.

"Well, unless you want some more water, I will let you go now. Thanks again for taking Gus off our hands. How was he, by the way?"

"Well, you know," Dr. Kelley appeared obtuse, "He IS a dog," he said, with extra emphasis on the word "is". "I am not exactly a dog fan, you know."

Char didn't believe her ears. *What did he mean, he wasn't a dog fan? This made no sense! Then why in the world had he offered to take Gus...surely if he wanted him out of the hospital he could have just called animal control or asked for a friend to come to pick him up, or something! This made no sense!* Char had assumed that because he took Gus home he must have had an affinity for dogs or something. So, what was really going on?

"What do you mean, you're not a dog fan?"

"I'm not," he said simply. "But I am becoming a Char fan. And I'll admit it, I thought it was kind of cute, the way you bumped into me and everything back at the hospital. You felt so bad, and I knew it was an accident. Oh, and by the way, I knew you weren't really homeless the entire time. The stalker part, I'm still not so sure about, however," he laughed, "Which is precisely why I'm not telling you where I live."

Char walked back to the living room and sat down. Once again, she couldn't believe what she was hearing. *Did this man ever say anything that made sense?* she began to wonder. Dr. Kelley followed her into the living room but remained standing.

"Look," he said. "What I really wanted was an excuse to come over here and see you. Since you are no longer my patient, I was wondering if you would like to go out with me sometime?" Char barely remembered more after that. When she came to, she was lying on the floor with Gus, sweating and smelling of dog. She would have to shower and change her clothes for the third time that day. She was so happy she didn't care. She would have done it 50 times if she needed to, to get to go on a date with Dr. Dreamy.

Chapter 35 - Duke

Duke woke up earlier than usual. The sun was not high enough in the sky to burn off the fog. It was grey, wet, and cloudy. It was still too cold to take a novice surfer without a wetsuit out for her first lesson. Instead, Duke grabbed a steaming hot cup of coffee from a fresh pot and sat down to keep an eye on the weather. As the sun continued to rise in the east, Duke hoped it would burn off the fog before he and Sofia headed out to Newport this morning for her first surf lesson. He wanted her to have a good time and knew that the weather would be a key factor. While he waited for the sun to rise and the weather to warm up, he got out the old surfboard that he seldom used and looked it over, making sure that it was still suitable. He felt responsible not only for her to have a good time, but to ensure her safety as well.

After both surfboards were loaded in the back of the Jeep and ready to go, there was nothing more to do than to climb back onto the couch and watch a little TV. Always looking for a warm place to sleep, it didn't take Bonkers long to climb up on Duke and settle in. Before long, both Bonkers and Duke were sound asleep, and it would have been difficult for anyone listening to tell who was snoring the loudest.

After several hours Duke awoke with a start, jumped off the couch, and looked outside. By now the fog had mostly burned off, and by the look of things, it was probably close to 11 a.m. For experienced surfers such as himself, 11 a.m. was far too late to head out for the best waves. Since Sofia was learning, 11 would be just fine, as he wanted her to be comfortable and a big wave was not the way to start anyway. Duke turned off the TV and stepped outside, and saw Sofia reading a magazine on her patio, her feet up, wearing her swimsuit and shorts. "About time there, big guy!" she teased.

Duke nervously ran his hand through his thick wavy hair before responding guiltily. He hadn't intended to be so late and didn't know how long she had been waiting. "Oh man, what is this, strike three?" he said. "I don't know what it is with you, I was up early but fell back asleep."

"Don't worry about it," she said. "Ready?" Sofia hopped up from the patio, slid her feet into her flip-flops, grabbed her towel along with her water bottle, and headed for the Jeep. Duke beat her to the door and opened it for her.

"Wow, thank you," she said, utterly impressed. She hadn't expected this kind of treatment, especially from Duke.

"Let's do this!" he said with an upbeat shout and playful grin. Duke turned on the radio and blasted some classic rock as they headed down Pacific Coast Highway toward Newport Beach.

The drive to the beach took about 15 minutes, but unfortunately, Duke wasn't accustomed to arriving at the beach this late in the day, and finding a parking spot took longer than the drive to get there. It was close to noon when they unloaded the car and headed down to the water. Duke kept glancing at Sofia, who appeared both eager and anxious at the same time. Duke smiled watching her. It had been a long time since he had taught someone to surf, but he remembered that feeling of being excited and fearful at the same time, that feeling that all new surfers experience.

"All right," he said. "Throw down your surfboard right here in the sand and hop on."

Sofia looked from the beach to the water, and back to the beach again, and then up at Duke. Duke stood there patiently waiting for her to stand on the surfboard, not quite understanding the hesitation. *If she's scared now,* he thought, *just wait until I get her in the water.* Sofia was never one to pass up an opportunity for a good tease, so finally she spoke up. "So maybe when I said I wanted to learn to surf, I wasn't clear..." she began. "I was kind of hoping we could surf in, you know, uh...the water?"

"Very funny. Actually, I did know that," he said, "but that is the second part of your lesson. The first part is teaching you to perform the techniques on the beach where the ground is stable. It won't be that way once you try it out there," he pointed toward the ocean, which now had several swells coming back to back towards the shoreline.

"What are you waiting for anyway?" he bantered. "You aren't scared, are you?"

"No," Sofia lied. "Okay, maybe a little," she admitted. It had been a long time since she had been to the beach other than to lay on the sand, and right now she wasn't even sure she could remember how to body surf.

"Tell ya what," Duke said. "I am going to give you a little incentive to help you overcome your fear. Most people aren't able to get up on the board on their first time out. If you do, we can stop and I'll buy you dinner on the way home. If you don't, you owe me. Deal?"

"Deal." Sofia picked up the surfboard and began carrying it toward the other surfers who were already in the water. "Come on," she called. "We don't have all day. If you're going to buy me dinner, I'm going to have to get started!" And with that she jumped into the waves, pushing her surfboard ahead of her as she went.

Well, Duke thought as he trailed behind her, *even though she is the oldest surfer I've ever had the privilege of teaching, she most certainly isn't the most difficult.* "Wait up!" he called after her, just in time to duck under an incoming wave. For the next few minutes a series of waves came by, and Duke was tempted to surf one in but thought better of it in case Sofia needed him for something. It was too soon for her to ride one in, as she was going to need Duke to talk her through it. By the time they were ready and in position, the swells had passed. It would be close to an hour before another round of waves would make another appearance. This gave Duke and Sofia plenty of time to hang out on their surfboards and talk.

At first, the conversation was light, Duke sharing tips about how to get up on the surfboard, and when she should start paddling if a wave should arrive. She practiced getting up on the surfboard while the water was still, and after practicing this repeatedly decided to take a rest.

"So tell me," Duke said after a few minutes. "What are you really doing out here with me, freezing to death, pretending to learn to surf?"

"I'm not pretending!" Sofia exclaimed, hurt. "I really do want to learn! But hey, if you want to go, we can leave," she said.

"No, no, that's not what I'm saying," he said. "I, I'm just surprised that you wanted to spend your free time with me, hanging out in this cold water. You don't even have a wetsuit. Don't you have a boyfriend or someone you'd rather hang out with?"

"No, no boyfriend to speak of..." Sofia said cautiously. Telling Duke, or anyone for that matter, about Katrina, was not something Sofia was ready for. But something about Duke felt different today, and she suddenly realized that she did want to talk about it. She felt as though they were on their own little islands out in the water, despite being in one of the most populous cities in California, and Sofia realized she really could use a friend. All sorts of thoughts began to race through her mind. *Could I trust him? What would he think? I mean, this was a very conservative county after all. And look what happened the last time I spent any time with him. He blabbed about me in a disparaging way all over the radio.* Every fiber of her being told her this was a bad idea.

She lay on her surfboard quietly, trying to think how to respond, when Duke broke the silence.

"Look," he said, "I didn't mean to pry. It's your business really. I was just making conversation, you know, to pass the time."

"You mean you aren't trying to find some dirt on me for your next radio show?" she blurted. *Ouch.* That came out harsher than she meant it. She could see by the look on his face that her comment had stung him, and she instantly regretted it. "I'm sorry," she said before he could utter another word.

"No, no, I get it," he said. "It's all right, really, it is..."

"I don't have a boyfriend, okay Duke? The truth is...I'm dating...a woman."

There. She'd said it. It was out there. Sofia sat quietly on her surfboard, waiting for his reaction. She felt like she had when she had been a young girl, swimming in her pool, stubbornly dipping her head underwater and swimming to the bottom to avoid hearing what anyone was saying, acting as if she didn't know someone was trying to talk to her, when she knew full well her sister, her mom, someone, was trying to get her attention. She briefly thought about diving off her surfboard and swimming down far beneath the waves to avoid hearing what he would say. But she was big now. She was an adult. She knew that would be rude, and as much as she wanted to, she wouldn't allow herself to do it. *No*, she thought. She would stay here and force herself to hear the reaction...

Chapter 36 - Valerie

This was the most exciting news Valerie had heard in ages! She couldn't believe it, Dr. Dreamy...and Char? "Char, I can't believe it!" she squealed with delight into her phone. "Seriously! No offense, but I thought he thought you were a homeless felon with stalker tendencies! How did it go from that to this?"

"I don't know, Val! Honestly, I still can't believe this is happening! I wish you were here so you could pinch me! Speaking of, when are you coming home?"

"I don't know for sure," Val admitted, "but hopefully soon. I think if I don't have any more setbacks and continue to improve, perhaps in the next few days. I am really getting eager to get the heck out of here. But I do want to thank you. I really think that having you in here with me boosted my spirits and had a positive effect on my healing."

"The pleasure was all mine, Val!" Char didn't even try to hide her elation. "Actually, I need to thank you! If it weren't for you, I would have never bumped into Dr. Dreamy, and I never would have been asked out by him! I can hardly believe it!"

And that was the way their friendship had always seemed to work. Just like any relationship with mutual reciprocity, each needed the other and both benefitted as a result. Both women were better off for having one another in their lives. The two were symbiotic, like flowers and bees, the sun and the rain, or Santa and his reindeer.

"As long as we're thanking each other," Val said, "that reminds me. We need to get back on track with our workouts—then we will be able to thank each other once again! You for your amazing body that you'll be able to dazzle Dr. Dreamy with, and me, for the money you'll give me to help pay for some of these medical bills I've incurred."

"I was afraid you were going to say that, Val," Char laughed. "But I'm also very happy you said that. It means you're getting better. I better hop on it sooner than later so the torture will be more bearable! Perhaps I will take Gus, or rather, Gus will take me, on another run around the island today."

"Right!" Val perked up. "And while you're at it throw in some push-ups. I want you to do three sets of 10 each, make sure to stretch properly before and after."

"Okay, okay, ease up there, trainer Bob!" The two friends laughed at the reference to the trainer who had been on the TV show *The Biggest Loser.* "We need to get you out of here first!" Char then felt panic run through her as reality set in. "Val, you HAVE to get out of the hospital, I mean, I don't mean to be selfish, but you have to help me get ready for my date with Dr. Kelley!

What will I wear? Who will do my hair? What will I say? How will I know if I should..."

Ever the voice of reason, Valerie cut her off before she could spiral any more than she already had in the past 30 seconds. "Char, take a deep breath. You will be fine. Remember, stay positive, think positive. You got this." Valerie could hear her friend's breathing begin to slow on the other end of the phone. She was settling down just as quickly as she had revved herself up.

"Okay, okay, yes...you are right. Okay. Besides, I don't even know when we are going yet. He didn't say."

"Remember," Valerie reminded her. "The most important thing is to stay positive. I've always known that, but being in the hospital like this and being, well, quite frankly, sicker than I've ever been, has caused me to take stock. I can now see firsthand just how important it is to remain positive under all circumstances. What you believe in your head will impact your body and everything else in your life. Don't forget that."

"Thanks, friend," Char said. "I can always count on you. I'm going to start calling you not just my coach, but my life coach!"

Valerie smiled at the compliment, thinking again about how lucky the two friends were. Their relationship was truly a symbiotic one. With that, the two friends hung up, and Valerie was soon fast asleep, dreaming contented and blissful dreams.

Chapter 37 - Sofia

Sofia replayed the day over and over and over in her head. She had heard of OCD as something negative. She had never heard of OCD, or obsessive-compulsive disorder, as being a *good* thing. But that was *EXACTLY* what it was: happy OCD! *Why didn't anyone ever talk about that?* she wondered. How did it happen? She kept playing the events of the day over and. over. She had willed herself not to make the same mistake she had made the first time. She was going to keep things strictly on a friendship basis. She knew just how rare it was to be given a second chance and she had promised herself that no way was she going to blow it. She had it all mapped out in her head, how she would behave, etc., etc. And yet, it had happened! And it wasn't terrible! In fact, it was...fabulous! She kept thinking that this truly was something that was beyond the physical realm. It was something in "the air," something they both felt, and couldn't deny, despite them both willing themselves to deny their feelings. For Sofia, she was commanding herself to deny her feelings out of respect and job security. Meaning, she didn't want to be fired. For Katrina, it had been the same. She had tried to force herself to look the other way because, at the end of the day, she was Sofia's boss. And everyone knew that office romances seldom worked out, and this one, in particular, had all of the odds stacked against it. First of all, she was Sofia's boss. Boom! Second, Sofia had always been straight, which meant this was, by definition, an experiment, and experiments often fail. What if this was some sort of experiment for Sofia and she decided after a few dates that she really wasn't into Katrina, or women for that matter, at all? Katrina could be setting herself up for a sexual harassment claim which she wouldn't be able to deny. Boom! Boom!

And yet...this undeniable pull, this feeling that was in the air, it had been tangible. You could almost see the air in between them as this jet trail, running horizontally between them, connecting them in an ethereal way that seemed spiritually ordained. And this is why, despite their best intentions, it had simply happened. There was no other explanation. It was beyond delightful.

It didn't matter what the rest of the world thought. It was there, ordained by the universe, and fuck what anyone else thought. If anyone had a problem with them, it was simply their problem. And this is why it felt so magical. Hence, the loop in Sofia's brain went round and round and round.

And as far as the attraction? It hadn't mattered that Katrina was a woman. Sofia interpreted this as further proof that the attraction was beyond the physical world. Which could only mean one thing: it was a spiritual connection. And how many people were ever this fortunate? It was something to Sofia that was all of a sudden everything.

Sofia knew that in following her heart, she was putting it all on the line. She also knew it was worth the risk. It takes an incredible amount of courage and bravery to follow your own knowing, your own heart, to what is unique and true for you and you alone. From the time we are small, society puts us in boxes. The boxes for women tell us how to act, what size we should be, who to marry. Women in particular are taught to be selfless and to put everyone else first. Sofia remembered how she had spent much of her early life not knowing who she was, as her energy had been spent trying to seek the approval of everyone around her. That meant she didn't even know who she was, other than to define herself, her personality, by who was in her presence. Who was she when no one else was around?

Over the years she gained confidence, became her own person, and began to be comfortable with who she was. But this escalated that to a new level. People knew who she was. And she was confident that no one saw this coming, including her. It would be her biggest act of bravery and courage yet. There were her children to consider, her friends, her reputation. She lived in Orange County: rich, Republican, and straight. She had close friends who were deeply religious and believed it was a sin to lay with the same sex and likened it to a murderer. "Just as a murderer shouldn't act on their feelings to kill," her friend had once said, "nor should a gay person act on their feelings."

Had Sofia really changed, or was she just taking the next natural step in honoring her true self, and having the courage to do it?

Chapter 38 - Char

Char had received the call around 11:30 a.m., just as she was starting to think about lunch.

Valerie was finally being discharged. This was fantastic news that couldn't have come at a worse time. Char was behind at work due to her own stint in the hospital, her house was a mess, and she still hadn't gotten around to going for a run with Gus. Still, without hesitation, she dropped everything except her keys, which she promptly picked up, and hopped in the car. These were the times when she especially valued being able to work from home, a privilege that she hadn't had prior to Covid. Perhaps she could make a case, if she performed well, to continue working from home even after Covid was finally under control and things appeared to return to normal.

As she pulled up to the hospital she grabbed her mass of hair and twisted it into a bun, trying to make herself as presentable as possible. *Why is it that every time I show up at this hospital*

I can't help but look disheveled? Char parked her car in the patient entrance and went in to get Valerie. She temporarily panicked when she saw the same security guard that had chased her the last time she was there. *Maybe he won't remember me?* she asked no one in particular. Unfortunately, she could tell by his downtrodden expression that he indeed had recognized her. But she put on her best smile, brushed a wisp of hair from her brow so she could be clearly seen, and pulled out her ID without even being asked. The security officer held onto her card for what seemed like an extraordinarily long amount of time, studying it. He glanced at her a few times before slowly handing it back to her and waving her through. Char let out a long breath that she hadn't realized she had been holding and took off toward the room she had only recently shared with Valerie.

As expected, when she entered the room the first thing she noticed was Valerie, who was wearing the world's biggest smile. "Hi, Char!" she beamed. "Thanks for coming! I am so excited to get out of here!"

"Absolutely," she looked around slyly, head down, with her hand shading her forehead.

"Now, uh, let's get out of here, okay? I don't want Dr. Kelley to see me looking like this...again! He might just change his mind about that date we set up. I sure hope he isn't working today."

"Okay, yeah. I just have to wait for my discharge papers, then we can bounce."

"No problem. I'll just go head out by the lobby and wait for you." And with that, Char picked up her purse and left the room. She was leaning against a wall in the lobby, checking her cell phone when she heard a familiar voice. She lifted her eyes from her phone just in time to see none other than Dr. Kelley, talking to one of the nurses at the nurses' station. *Hurry up, Val!* she pleaded. *Come on! He's gonna see me. No. Oh my god, this is so embarrassing.* And with that, she decided she was done waiting. She looked around desperately for a place to escape—and fast. She saw nowhere to go. To the left were the nurses' station, Valerie, and Dr. Kelley. To the right, near the entrance, were the security office, lobby doors, and check-in. Her choices were to go towards the nurses' station where she would surely be seen, or to run out of the lobby to the parking lot, leaving Valerie to her own devices and wondering where Char went. *Think, think, think*, she pleaded. Suddenly, out of nowhere, she saw a door across the lobby, somewhere she could hide out of sight until Val had checked out. This way, she could help Valerie out but not be seen by Dr. Kelley while she was still looking grungy, again.

She ran on her tiptoes, bent over to make herself unseen and as small as possible, and checked the door handle. *Yes!* As luck would have it, she finally caught a break in this darned hospital. Without wasting any time, she flew open the door just enough to slip inside, and closed it behind her. Once in there, she realized it was super cramped and dark. She looked around for a light switch so she could turn on the light to see where she was, but couldn't find one. She gave up on that and began feeling around a table, and desk, to try and "see" with her hands. Unfortunately, her hand was accidentally submerged in a pail of dirty mop water, which told her she had found the broom closet or maintenance room. *Eeeewww!* She shrieked, wiping her hand on her clothes. She stood quietly for a few more moments, trapped in the dark, with nowhere to move. She grabbed her cell phone and was attempting to text Valerie when the door opened. She looked up, and standing in front of her with a grimace on his unfriendly face, was...you guessed it.

The security guard that she had evaded the first time in the hospital. The same one that now resented letting her into the hospital today.

Char thought fast. She had no other option. There was no guarantee, but it used to work. It had been a long time since she had tried it, but she was literally backed up against a wall and could think of nothing else to do: she would have to flirt.

Char cocked her head to one side as she simultaneously batted her eyes and flashed her most innocent smile. "Oh, hi, officer! Thank goodness you are here! Ha..." She made a meager attempt at a laugh. "I was looking for the restroom. I guess I took a wrong turn!"

The officer wasn't buying it, but he decided to have a little fun with her anyway. "Yes, I understand ma'am. That would be confusing. You might want to try the door that reads, 'Women' on the outside. Common mistake...I can certainly see why you were confused."

"Right...right..." Char replied. She knew by his sarcasm that this wasn't working. So she did what had seemed to work for her the last time she was in this mess. She took a deep breath, held tight to her purse, and, pushing past Mr. Security, ran like the wind towards the parking lot.

Chapter 39 - Duke

Duke finally spoke after what felt to Sofia like an eternity in which she was being judged.

"Well, I will admit I didn't see that coming," Duke said. "I mean, I hate to be judgmental, but you don't exactly come close to fitting the stereotypical lesbian, you know? No offense. But hey, it's whatever. No big deal."

Sofia dove below the water, not to avoid hearing the already spoken words, but to wash the tears away that were welling up in her eyes.

Duke waited patiently, wondering nervously if he'd inadvertently said something to insult her once again. This honest dialogue, this baring your soul kind of stuff was new to him and made him uncomfortable. In fact, they were both out of their comfort zone. For Sofia, it was hearing herself reveal an identity she'd never imagined for herself. Daughter, mother, teacher, wife, principal, and athlete, sure. Lesbian? Gay? Bi or bi-curious? Absolutely not on the radar. Not even a little. So hearing her admit it out loud was foreign to her own ears. She was trying it on, here, in the middle of the ocean, where no one but Duke could hear.

Duke, on the other hand, was out of his comfort zone too. Here he was, half-naked, in the water, with a woman that he wasn't trying to date. They were talking about their feelings, and he was sincerely trying to say the right thing and be supportive. He was so used to being "the wise guy," the guy that knew how to rile everyone up, that being sincere and sensitive was actually difficult. He was so good at it, in fact, that he made his living off of it. He also thought about diving under the water to escape, or better yet, riding the next big wave into the beach and waiting for her there. But there was a part of him that welcomed this opportunity too. As uncomfortable as it was, he knew he had wanted to make a change. He had slept with countless women but had never had a satisfying relationship. He wanted things to be deeper if he was ever going to settle down permanently. Perhaps he could "experiment" with Sofia, see how it felt, learn how to really communicate, without the pressure of sex. Since she wasn't available romantically anyway, perhaps it would be the perfect opportunity to try a new way of relating to women. When Sofia finally emerged from below the surface of the water, Duke, who made a living talking, was struggling to figure out what to say. After staring at Sofia, the beach, and everything else, he glanced sideways at Sofia. After a few moments, he finally found the nerve to look at her, directly this time, and ask, "So, what's it like? Do you still like men? If I'm prying I can stop. I am really trying to separate myself from being a radio talk show host and a guy who screws up by using nice neighbors such as you as radio fodder. If you trust me, it won't go any further."

Sofia returned his gaze and looked him directly in the eye. Duke could see her face tense and then soften before she answered with a nod, never diverting her eyes from his. "I do," she said.

This was a first for Duke, and it felt good. Suddenly, he wanted to be there for Sofia and realized he didn't want anything in return other than her trust and friendship. It would be such a compliment, such a great feeling, to be trusted, and to not have any ulterior motive. And although he didn't entirely understand it, he wasn't homophobic either. Perhaps this would broaden his understanding too. After all, the world needs more acceptance right now, not less. He knew her story was off-limits right now, but perhaps down the road, he would be able to use his platform to educate, to bring people together, rather than simply create cheap and meaningless sensational talk radio. He made a silent vow to himself that he wouldn't screw this up. Suddenly, it became very important to Duke that he would protect her. He knew this was a big deal, and he knew he was probably the only person she had told thus far. He took it as a compliment and decided to protect not only the disclosure but whatever she was going through as well. This was the start of a new and more sensitive Duke.

Finally, the sun began to set and the air felt cool on their skin. Duke noticed goosebumps forming on Sofia's arms and back, and suggested they call it a day. Although Sofia had wanted to try to get up on one more wave (that would bring her total to two times that day, two and a half if you count the time she stood up but then immediately fell off the backside), she agreed and headed for shore. She was too tired to race anymore and was cold and hungry, with the taste of saltwater forming a gritty paste along her lips. Her eyes burned as well, and wiping them with sandy hands only aggravated the situation. Despite her minor physical annoyances, her spirit was calm and content. She felt proud of pushing herself beyond her former comfort zones and was ready to call it a day. She was relieved when she got to the shore and Duke offered to carry her board up to the Jeep for her. She carried her sandy towel behind her as she followed him to the Jeep. The towel now felt heavy in her arms, weighed down by the water and sand it had absorbed during the day.

Sofia was just thinking about dinner...*what should I have?* when Duke turned off the main highway toward the little island and turned instead toward Corona del Mar.

"Uh, I hate to be a backseat driver, but this isn't the way home," she said. "Where are we going?"

"Did that saltwater wash all of your brains out of your head? Look, a promise is a promise, so I'm taking you to dinner! After all, you did manage to get up on the board today. You earned it!"

Sofia smiled at his thoughtfulness and felt happy. Inwardly, she couldn't help but laugh at the turn of events in her life. Up until now, her "friends" had all been female, and her boyfriends had been, well, boys. And now, here she was, feeling as though she was making a genuine new friend who happened to be male, while her partner (or so she hoped) was suddenly female. "Never say never!" she smiled as they pulled into a rustic yet bucolic Mexican restaurant just yards from the beach.

Duke grinned. "You like Mexican?"

They had just sat down to eat at the little bar that overlooked the ocean with the setting sun and Sofia asked, "What about you, Duke? It's your turn now. You heard all about me, what's your story?"

Duke could feel his heart beating faster and the blood rushing to his scalp as he grew nervous. *All right,* he thought, *now this is going way too far, way too fast. Getting drunk and making out with some girl I barely know is one thing. But telling my life story to someone I might possibly see again? Sober? Yeah, no.*

But Duke wanted to grow as a person. And he didn't want to be a jerk. So he thought he could take a baby step and talk, honestly. To a girl. About the truth. Himself. But first, there was just one thing he needed to help this plane get off the ground.

"Bartender," he called, "another beer, please. Oh, and can I get a double shot of tequila?" The music in the background was playing the stereotypical mariachi music, and Duke found it hard to concentrate. The bartender placed a bottle of beer with a lime in front of him, followed by a double shot of

Jose Cuervo. After downing the shot and taking a long swig of his beer, he responded.

"Alright," he said. "If you really want to know...here it goes..."

Chapter 40 - Katrina

Katrina woke up the next day with a smile, her thoughts turning instantly to Sofia. She was in love, and she knew it. There was no turning back, which meant she just needed to be careful. Depending on how things went, she would look for another job at the end of the year. She knew she couldn't continue to be Sofia's boss as well as her partner. This was a huge risk, and the sooner she separated her personal life from her professional one, the better. Katrina then stopped herself suddenly from this line of thinking. *What the hell?* she asked herself. She was getting way too ahead of herself. They had just officially begun their relationship, and she was already thinking about looking for a new job? For all she knew, Sofia was going through an experimental phase and would probably tire of the whole thing within a few months. It was hard, but she didn't want to get hurt again. She already knew how she felt and knew herself well enough to know that it was unlikely her feelings would change. But Sofia was another story. This was new for Sofia, she had just gotten divorced, etc. This relationship (could she even call it that yet?) had all the trappings of a fling: it was a rebound for Sofia, who had always been straight, who was at the prime time to be going through a midlife crisis. Even her own children had intimated as much. So many variables could come between them. *No, it was better to try to take things slow,* she concluded logically.

But for once, Katrina's logical side was no match for her emotional side. At 55, she knew what she wanted, and she had already opened the door that risked everything. Preventing herself from getting carried away was going to be challenging. She felt as though Sofia was exactly who she had been waiting for. She was the woman of her dreams, so to speak, and she couldn't wait to spend forever with her. She had always heard of people knowing when they met "the one," but at 55, Katrina was beginning to give up on that happening to her. She was now beginning to rethink everything. Perhaps her time was still yet to come.

And with that happy thought, Katrina finished getting ready for work, eager to start her day and see Sofia. She thought about asking her to dinner, perhaps some golfing this weekend, maybe a little wine. Katrina couldn't remember the last time she had felt so happy. She was finally finding her person, much later in life than most. Perhaps this is what made it all the sweeter. *And what about Sofia?* she mused. Sofia was supposed to have been married forever. A soft, contented smile spread across her face as she pet Annie. *Yes,* she thought to herself, *I had to wait a long time for this, but we are so lucky!* Katrina couldn't get over how happy she was for the first time in her life, a love she knew had started late in life but would ultimately end up lasting forever. And with that, she gave Annie an extra stroke, noted how soft she felt, and headed out the door.

Chapter 41 - Valerie

It had never felt so good to be home! Although weakened, Valerie found the strength to open all the windows in her house and let the cool breeze from the Pacific waft through her house. She had transparent cotton drapes that blew vertically into the house rhythmically in time with each swell of the waves just outside her window. It felt to her as an extension of the water, right through into her house, and she loved it. This would be the perfect place to recover, surrounded by things that she loved, the beautiful view just outside her window. It was nearly springtime now and her pink hibiscus was beginning to bloom, as were the orange bougainvillea that she loved so much. She settled onto her couch and looked out the window. There she saw various beachgoers assembling on the sand, some engaged in a game of volleyball. The smell of coconut sunblock and barbecue entered her house with the breeze. She could hear the voices of people on the beach, and screams of delight from children as they played in the water. An occasional rock song that she recognized entered her house as well, as sunbathers listened on their radios and boomboxes. Always looking for the silver lining, Valerie realized that she appreciated all of this now more than ever. Had she taken it all for granted before she fell ill? She just hadn't anticipated how much she missed all of these sights and sounds that delighted her senses.

Gus also appeared happy to be home, as he couldn't decide where he'd rather be, outside basking in the sun like the beachgoers, or inside snuggled next to Val. Being unable to make up his mind, he spent most of the afternoon going in and out the dog door, first checking out the action outside, laying down, then getting up and coming back inside to plop himself down on the couch next to Val, and so on and so forth. Both felt very content to not only be home but to be home together.

The only disappointment was that Valerie hadn't felt up to going to Char's house to watch her get ready for her date with Dr. Kelley. The two had talked about it endlessly, debating every detail of her outfit down to the precise shade of lipstick that she ought to wear. Valerie was so grateful for Char's help and support these past few months, especially when she was in the hospital, caring for Gus and all. She really wanted to be there to help her get dressed for her date.

"Okay, okay, okay!" Valerie had made Char promise she would tell her every detail short of videotaping it. Truth be told, a secret videotape of the evening would have been preferred, but

Valerie didn't want to be unreasonable. Char promised she would get the entire play by play, no matter how late it was when she got home.

"Okay, one more time!" Valerie couldn't help herself. "You must tell me everything, and I don't want you leaving out one detail!"

"I know, I know, Val!" Char was desperate to get off the phone. "I gotta go! He is going to be here in 15 minutes and right now I am still standing here in my underwear!"

With that, Valerie heard a click and saw that her call had ended. She was left holding her phone in her hand needlessly. With nothing further left to say since Char had clearly ended the call, Valerie tossed her phone on her bed and resumed tidying up her house. Next, she decided to turn on a movie, anxious to relax and pass the time until she got a call from Char after the date.

Chapter 42 - Duke

As was unusually uncommon for Duke, the snide-talking, pot-stirring radio personality was speechless. Duke finished the bottom of his beer, signaled for another, and sheepishly asked,

"So, uh, what is it that you want to know?"

Sofia smiled to herself and realized she quite liked the fact that the tables were now turned.

She took another sip of her drink, rum, and coke, and replied, "You. Anything. I want you to tell me something about you. The REAL you. Not the radio Duke, not Mr. Goodtime Guy Duke, the genuine, authentic your-pain-is-real Duke. What's he like?"

Duke looked at her, then looked back down at his empty bottle, stalling. He wanted to do this, he needed to do this, he even owed it to her, he reasoned. Still, it was difficult. He was not used to opening up to anyone.

"Oh, man. Shit. Okay, well here goes I guess. So I was born in northern California and I have an older brother. Is that what you want to hear?"

Laughing quietly, Sofia tried to respond encouragingly. "Maybe you can fast forward, just a bit," she said.

"Okay, okay. Uh, man. This is hard."

"Tell me about your first love," Sofia nudged.

"All right. So, I had just finished high school. We met in chemistry class."

"What's her name?"

"Valerie."

Sofia froze. There was only one Valerie that she knew. It wasn't that common of a name.

Surely it couldn't be the same Valerie, the one that she knew...

"What's her last name?" Sofia was dying to know.

"Parker."

Sofia couldn't believe her ears!

"You mean the same Valerie Parker? The one who used to be a chef, and is really into fitness and just got out of the hospital?"

"She was in the hospital?" Duke couldn't believe his ears. "Is she okay?"

"Wait, hold on," Sofia interjected, before responding. "Are we talking about the same Valerie Parker? A northern California transplant who moved down here after college?"

"Yes, that's Valerie!" Duke said, astonished.

"Is she okay? You mean she was in the hospital? Oh my god. I had literally lost touch with her after our breakup, except for one fateful evening that didn't go so well. I, uh, didn't know she was in the hospital. Is she going to be all right?"

"Well, yes, she's out now. I don't know her personally, but my good friend Char and her are best friends. I was going to start working out with Val as my personal trainer until she got sick.

But yeah, she's okay. She had pancreatitis or something like that, I heard."

Duke couldn't believe his ears. What a small world. He never had completely lost his feelings for Valerie, but he'd given up after he'd fucked it up so badly...

Impatient, Sofia implored him. "So, tell me! What happened?"

Duke took another swig of his beer, which was just about empty already, and shook his head in disbelief. "Wow, I had no idea," he said. "Anyway, we met in high school chemistry and I was instantly attracted to her. But I was shy and awkward back then, not the babe magnet that I am today," he laughed.

Sofia rolled her eyes and played along. "I'm listening."

"Well, there's really not that much to tell. Okay, okay, so Valerie was super beautiful, you know? Like the 'All-American' just got off a horse, Ralph Lauren kind of beautiful, right? Straight golden brown hair, past her shoulders, real natural-looking. She was really sweet too. Anyway, all year long, I pined for her. But it took me forever to get the courage to ask her out."

"How come?"

"Look at me, Sofia. I mean, I joke about my charm and good looks, etc., and I've really increased my confidence over the years, but back then, I was kind of a partier, class clown, going nowhere kind of a guy. I think we both knew she was too good for me. You know? She was smart, sweet, played sports, and really was an all-around great person. Mature. Very mature. And poised. I think she was even in student government."

"So what happened?"

"Well, I went out with my friends one night, and we ran into her at some ice cream shop. My friends knew that I'd liked her the entire year, and they dared me to go up to her and ask her out."

"Did you?"

"Not at first. But then I thought about it, and I thought to myself, 'Fuck. Get some balls dude. It's the end of the year. You may not ever have another chance.'"

"What did she say?"

"She said no."

"Really?" Sofia brought her hand to her mouth and tried to cover her surprise, her eyebrows raised in shock and horror. "Oh my god! You poor thing! What did you do?" "I'm just kidding, she said yes," Duke laughed.

"You jerk!" Sofia slapped his shoulder. "So what happened?"

"Well, things went really well for a while. We went out a couple of times. Had a great time, nothing too serious. I really, really cared for her. Was starting to fall for her even. But then school ended and I moved down here. She stayed on and went to Berkeley. She didn't actually move down to SoCal until after college. So you know, we broke up. That's basically it."

"That's it? That's so sad! Did you keep in touch with her? Have you ever seen her since she's moved down here?"

"Yeah, that's the part that sucks. We went out to dinner once after she'd moved down here. I screwed it up. I acted like a real jerk. I wanted to prove to her that I cleaned up my act since high school, so to speak. I acted like a pompous, arrogant asshole. I boasted about my radio show and having made something of myself. I paid no attention to her or her accomplishments. I didn't intend to, but I overdid it. I came across as a jerk. I guess you could say I was trying too hard.

Anyway, it backfired. She left right after dinner and I knew I wouldn't hear from her again."

"So did you ever hear from her again?"

"Eh, no. I tried to call her a few times, but she blocked my calls. Ever since then, I never get too close to anyone, really. I guess it just hurts too much. I just feel like such a screw-up that it's easier to just go with the 'tough guy' image. The 'love 'em and leave 'em' type, you know?

Come on," he said, standing up and reaching for my chair. "Let's get outta here."

Chapter 43 - Char

Char was standing next to her ironing board, trying to remember how to iron without adding more wrinkles to her skirt and blouse. She was very clear on the concept of ironing. It was the execution where she was coming up short. "Shit!" She had let the words escape her lips without thinking. Char hadn't worn this outfit in quite some time because she hated ironing so much, but the blue pencil skirt and loose-fitting peach-colored blouse were what she had wanted to wear tonight. If she remembered correctly, the outfit was flattering in both its slimming effect and hue and so she decided it would be worth the time it would take her to iron it. That was if she could iron it successfully. At five minutes to six, still in her underwear, her doorbell rang, followed by a quick *rap, rap, rap* at the door. *Oh my god!* she screamed to herself. *He can't be here!* Char took one look at her bare legs and skirt, still draped over the ironing board, and panicked.

"Hang on," she called, trying to sound calm. "I'm coming!" She was out of time and so quickly unplugged her iron, leaving the skirt still hanging over the board. She ran back to her room, looked around, and found a pair of jeans on the floor in the corner by her bed, still inside out and in a heap from the last time she had worn them. "One second!" she called again, not wanting him to leave. "Hang on..." She turned her jeans so that they had the right side in, ran her arm across them in an attempt to flatten the wrinkles that had formed in them, and grabbed her body spray. She sprayed two squirts on her jeans, hoping it would freshen them. She yanked them on as she headed to the door, still barefoot. At least she had managed to iron her blouse before the doorbell had rung. The doorbell was ringing for the third time when Char finally managed to reach it. She swung it open and there was Dr. Kelley, holding a stuffed animal, a dog, in his hand. He handed it to her.

"I thought you might need something to keep you company, now that you're no longer watching Gus," he said. Char was speechless as she reached out to take the fluffy German shepherd that Dr. Kelley was holding out to her. It was incredibly soft, and a whole lot lighter than Gus had been. Char was truly touched by the thoughtful gesture.

"Thanks!" she said, genuinely meaning it. "Come in." Char took a moment to see if she was appropriately dressed now that Dr. Kelley was here. She all of a sudden realized that she didn't know what she should call him. In fact, come to think of it, did she even know his first name? She tried to picture his name tag at work. All she could remember was Dr. Kelley, and of course, her secret name for him, Dr. Dreamy. That would never do. She dismissed the thought and decided to err on the side of caution. She would avoid using his name, or if pressed, default to the more formal Dr. Kelley, and wait to see if he corrected her.

Char held tight to her new stuffed dog, still thinking about names. "So does he have a name?" she asked.

Dr. Kelley smiled. "I thought I'd let you name her. Or him. I'm not really sure if he is a he or a she. So I guess you get to choose. But I did look into his pedigree, and in addition to having great bloodlines, he has impeccable manners. He doesn't bark or pull on a leash, so you should be safe there. Also, he likes lazing around the house, so you'll never have to worry about him dragging you through the hospital the way Gus did."

"That's true," Char smiled, playing along. "But maybe I like that Gus dragged me through the hospital," she said coyly.

"Why would that be?" Dr. Kelley asked incredulously, his left eyebrow raised higher than the right.

Char turned about and looked back over her right shoulder towards the door where Dr. Kelley was still standing, and said flirtatiously, "If it weren't for Gus tearing down the hospital corridor, I'd never have met you."

For the first time since they'd met, Dr. Kelley was at a loss for words. He stood frozen, with the door still open, and stared. Then, without warning, he walked over to her, grabbed the stuffed dog out of her arms, and placed it on the couch beside her. Still not saying a word, he held her gaze, and lunged towards her, pulling her in. In the next moment, he kissed her on the lips, still holding her in his arms.

"I don't even know your name," she whispered. She felt the heat rising up her neck and across her cheeks, revealing her blush.

"Well, well...Miss Char," he said in his best doctor voice, "you are appearing quite flushed, and I notice your heart is racing. Are you quite alright?"

Regaining her composure, Char looked him square in the eye, and repeated, "Excuse me, doctor, but I still don't know your first name."

Chapter 44 - Duke

Duke was about to see Valerie for the first time in about 10 years and was nervously prepping the barbecue for when she would arrive. His conversation with Sofia had stirred something deep within him, and he had reached out to see if he could make one final attempt to pick up where they had left off so many years ago. Not expecting much, Duke went online and sent Valerie a message.

"Heard about you being in the hospital. I just wanted to say 'hi' and hope you are okay. Call me sometime, if you want." He left his number at the end of his email.

Surprisingly, Valerie had responded, and the two talked on the phone a few days later. It had gone surprisingly well.

When Valerie arrived at Duke's house on Balboa Island almost 10 years after the last time he'd seen her, he was right back where he'd been when he first fell for her in high school. Yes, she looked a tad older. A few gray hairs framed her face and he could see where her hair dye had covered a few more that were growing out along her part. Her eyes had aged too, with a few prominent lines extending out toward her temples on each eye, followed by softer lines underneath. He wondered what changes she saw in him, and hoped that he had improved with age, like a fine wine or some bullshit like that. Overall though, she was still as lovely as ever and was so happy just to have a second (or in his case, third) chance after all these years.

"So, why did you agree to come over and have dinner with me tonight?" Duke wanted to know.

"I dunno," Valerie said. "I guess everything that's happened...the Covid pandemic, me being in the hospital, it just sort of, changes your perspective sometimes," she said. "Besides, I wanted to see if you really had improved with time," she teased.

"Got it. Good." She was no longer angry. She'd had a change of heart, and was willing to give him a third chance. It wasn't exactly a date, he thought, but still, he'd take it. The thought that he couldn't screw this up played round and round in his head, repeatedly, as he tried to make it sink in.

He resumed his barbecuing on the patio when the thought suddenly popped into his head.

"There's someone I want you to meet," he said, his thoughts turning back to his conversation with Sofia, and the influence their conversation had had on him.

"Okay," Valerie responded cautiously. "Um, I don't mean to offend you, and I know we're not 'spring chickens' anymore, so to speak, but isn't it a little early for that? I mean, I already met Bonkers. I don't think I am ready to take our friendship, or whatever you call this, to the next level, meet your parents, that sort of thing if that's what you're thinking."

Duke froze for a minute, staring at Valerie before he understood what she was saying.

"What? No, no, it's nothing like that," he said. "I just want you to meet a friend." "But you don't have any friends," she winked at him.

"Yeah, I deserved that," he said. "But Valerie, there's something you should know about me. I've changed. I'm not the same guy I was 10 years ago. I'm ready for a real relationship now. I see women differently than I used to. My friend, Sofia, has helped me to realize some things."

"Oh yeah? Like what?"

"Like that, I am ready to settle down, have a meaningful relationship with a woman, and that having a deeper relationship with a woman is more important than, well, you know..."

"Sex?"

"Yeah."

"Really? Or is this just your newest line to get me to go to bed with you? Come on Duke,

I'm not that stupid."

"No, I am really serious. And to prove it, I want you to meet her."

"Her? Your friend is a 'her'? I am not sure if I should be impressed or skeptical. You never were able to have a non-sexual relationship with a woman in the past. Are you sure?" Valerie asked, dubious. "How do I know you aren't already sleeping with her?" Valerie didn't completely trust that Duke had changed. "Now I would really like to meet this so-called 'friend' because I am going to straight-up ask her if you two have been, you know, intimate."

"No problem," Duke said with a smile. "I would like you to meet her too. But first, a toast. To us. To new beginnings. To picking up where we left off."

"To us," Valerie agreed, smiling.

They clinked glasses together and took a sip. Duke then chased his wine down with a few swigs from his beer, which he had thoughtfully placed on the table near his wine.

"Aaaah..." Duke let out a contented sigh and glanced from his plate of food (steak, green beans, and mashed potatoes) up to Valerie and back. He moved his food around his plate nervously, mingling his green beans with his potatoes in a haphazard manner, looking for his words. He felt different than he had on other dates, and every word that was about to emerge from his mouth he second-guessed, fearing he would sound like his old self. He wanted to drop the charade, the way he learned with Sofia. But with Sofia, it had been easier. He really liked Valerie, and that added pressure. He didn't want to give her the wrong impression and had gotten so used to his selfcentered and arrogant ways with other women that he had to choose his words carefully. He looked up and met her eyes, and gave her an awkward smile before focusing back on the arrangement of green beans and mashed potatoes.

After dinner, they walked the 10 steps over to Sofia's front door, and Duke started knocking when the door swung open. In surprise at having her open the door so quickly, Duke jumped.

"What were you doing? Spying on us?" he asked with a wink.

"Shut up," she said, laughing. "Of course not! I was actually just on my way out! I'm headed over to Katrina's for the evening. What's up?"

"Sofia, I would like you to meet someone special, Valerie. Valerie, this is Sofia." "It is so nice to meet you!" Sofia said, genuinely meaning it. She had heard so much about her through Char, and now, through Duke. Sofia would have already hired Valerie as her trainer if she hadn't fallen ill...

While Valerie and Sofia became acquainted, Duke popped back to his house next door and went inside to whip up a batch of margaritas. When he came back, Valerie and Sofia were sitting comfortably on the porch out front, watching the last of the day's sun as it set over Newport Harbor. There were a few people, children mostly, still lingering down on the sand by the water. The water was quietly lapping at the shore, the boats swelling up and down with the waves.

"You didn't tell me she was a lesbian!" Valerie laughed. "Okay, now I know you didn't sleep with her."

Duke just smiled.

"Or maybe, you are trying to get her to change her ways if you know what I mean?" "Hell no, Valerie! First of all, she's a lot older than me. Secondly, she is happy with her partner, Katrina. But most importantly, Valerie, I am, and always have been, wild about you." "Thanks," Valerie said, smiling. "Me too, but I'm still not sleeping with you. At least not tonight," she laughed.

Duke laughed too. He knew she was joking, and besides, he didn't care. He had known Valerie for about 20 years and knew he wanted to get it right this time. How could he prove to her that he'd changed if he tried to get her to sleep with him right away?

At this stage in his life, he had finally realized that there were more important things than having his immediate needs met. The most important thing to him was to not screw this up again. He had already been given more chances than most men would have had.

At the end of the evening, Duke walked Valerie to her car. He hugged her warmly and gave her a kiss goodbye, on the cheek. It wasn't so much what Duke had said that evening, but what he didn't say that had convinced Valerie that he had matured.

Duke walked back into his house, elated. He couldn't wait to tell Sofia everything.

Chapter 45 - Valerie

It was half-past eleven. She flipped through the TV channels again, trying to find something that would pique her interest. For a few minutes, she got sucked into one of those real crime-solving shows, before she thought better of it and decided that wouldn't be a good idea before bed. She then turned back to the nightly news. A reporter was talking about a similarly disturbing scene, of a hit and run that left one person seriously injured and another one running from the police, his whereabouts unknown. Valerie decided this wasn't much better than the crime show, and decided to turn off the TV completely. She looked at the time again and willed herself to stay awake. She and Char had made a pact that they would talk as soon as Char got home from her date with Dr. Kelley. *Things must be going well,* she thought to herself. She looked around the room, wondering how to occupy herself and stay awake until Valerie called. She decided to have a pre-midnight snack. She wandered over to the kitchen, opened the refrigerator, and took inventory of its contents: yogurt, eggs, milk, fruit, and some brown rice that had been leftover from last night's dinner. *Not exactly midnight snacking material,* she thought. She closed the refrigerator door and headed over to her bedroom, where Gus was already waiting for her, keeping her side of the bed warm.

"Scootch over, buddy," she said, shoving him over just enough so she could squeeze in next to him. Valerie climbed in next to him with good intentions of staying awake in a more comfortable fashion, but before long, the sound of Gus's contended breathing had soothed her and without realizing it, she too was soon snoozing right alongside him. By the time she awoke the next morning, she was still groggy and collecting her thoughts. *Why didn't I hear from Char last night? What happened?* She decided to check her phone. *Three missed calls?* She looked over at her text messages and saw that she had missed two from Char and one from Duke. The texts from Char had been sent to her around 3 a.m., whereas Duke had reached out to her early this morning before she was awake. *Wait! 3 a.m.?! No wonder I fell asleep!* Valerie sprang out of bed, calling

Gus after her. "Come on boy! Let's go!" She took Gus outside into the cool morning sea air to pee. Gus, who was happily jumping and spinning around without any coffee needed, was now ready to greet the day. Valerie, on the other hand, was thinking about going back to bed, but the thought of coffee and checking in with Char, and possibly Duke, redirected her.

Valerie grabbed her warm coffee and sat down on the couch to call Char, where the call went directly to voicemail. *Aaaarrgghh! Figures!* she thought to herself. She understood as it was still early. However, she was practically dying not knowing what had happened last night on Char's date. And there had been no hint of how it went on the voicemail that Char left. Unfortunately, Valerie would simply have no choice but to wait.

Chapter 46 - Char

It was after 4 p.m. when Char finally rolled out of bed, still in her nightgown, and wandered into the living room to peer out her window at the beachgoers and sunbathers enjoying the sunny day. As the thoughts of last night came ambling back to her, a slow, satisfied smile crept across her face and left her feeling very content. The evening had been absolutely wonderful. Char thought to herself about the series of events that had led up to last night: Valerie, the hospital, Gus getting loose, and her bumping into Dr. Kelley. Who knew that these events that felt so minuscule at the time could end up possibly changing her life...

Not that she wanted to get carried away, but one just never knew. There seemed to be limitless possibilities here on Balboa Island, and her friend Valerie had taught her time and again the benefit of positive thinking. Why couldn't she be a glass-half-full kind of person? Speaking of

Valerie, she suddenly realized she hadn't spoken to her in a good 13 hours since she had gotten home! *I better call her right now,* she thought.

Without any further hesitation, she picked up her cell and rang her best friend. "Hey Val!" she said. "You will never believe this. I had the most amazing night!"

Chapter 47 - Sofia

Sofia was all too familiar with the phrase "time flies when you're having fun". Today at work, she, unfortunately, learned the opposite was also true. She was so eager to go spend time with Kat after work that she thought the day would never end. She found herself in her office, lost in thought, thinking. It was hard to think about anything other than Katrina. She thought about love, courage, and following her heart. She thought about the world right now: divided, full of hate, the pandemic, and so on. She thought about how short life is, and how the world needed more of what she and Katrina had: love. If people wanted to judge them, so be it. She was thankful that at this stage of life she finally had enough self-confidence to do what felt right for her, despite what others thought. And this love with Katrina felt right. In fact, the world needed more love, more acceptance of all kinds, not just in terms of sexual preference but of race, religion...everything. It seemed that anyone or anything that was different was always subjected to criticism. She had had enough. She knew she couldn't change the world, but she could start with herself. She knew as long as she was putting love, rather than hate, into the world, it felt right, no matter what anyone else said or thought. She would not be so weak as to do what she had done in the past and be ruled by others' opinions of her. *Life was too short*, she said again to herself.

She knew she still had a long way to go. There were her boys to consider, her friends who were opposed to this lifestyle. And there was a general shock that she knew others, even if they were open-minded, would have at this unexpected news. At nearly 50 years old and having been on a specific and "straight" path for so long, it would be an about-face. Did she have the courage to turn her life and identity around? At this stage of the game, with life being so short, could she afford to not take the risk? The answer was no.

As Sofia rushed out after work to head over to Katrina's, she looked around her. Here she was, in Orange County, living on Balboa Island. She was living her childhood dream. She pulled up to Katrina's house and couldn't be happier. Just sitting on the couch together, arm in arm, spending time talking, laughing, and looking into one another's eyes felt like heaven. It was at that moment that Sofia realized, for the first time, that she had been wrong. The happiest place on earth is not a place. It is being with the one you love. And at that moment, Sofia shocked herself by admitting that yes, she did, in fact, feel like she loved Kat. Perhaps it was too soon to know for sure, but her heart had led her this far, and it was telling her this was the real deal. If it was real, and if it was love, then she also had to admit that her happiest place was with a loved one, wrapped in his (or her) arms, wherever that might be. Who would have thought that the man that was supposed to be the love of her life would ultimately end up being a woman?

End of Book 1

What will happen to Char and Dr. Kelley after their first official date? Will there be another date and possibly a relationship? Where will they live? Will there be a wedding? Children? Will Char continue the training that she had just started before Val got sick? Or will she "cash in" on her inheritance and move and reinvest in horse property, following in her mother's footsteps?

Find out what happens next in book two of the *Never Say Forever* series, *"Better Now Than Forever"*

Never Say Forever series:

1. *Better Late Than Forever*
2. *Better Now Than Forever*
3. *Better Before Than Forever*
4. *Better Never Than Forever*
5. *Better After and Forever*

If you liked this book... please be so kind as to post a review! It helps new authors (like me!) to get my books out in front of readers. **Or...**

...Keep in touch! I can be found online at the following locations:

Website: shelleytan.com

Twitter: @shelleytan1

Facebook: Shelley Tan

To receive a monthly free subscription to my newsletter, send an email to: **shelleytanauthor@gmail.com** and type **"newsletter signup"** in the subject line, to be sure to be notified of new releases and more information!

(You can also follow me on Amazon, and get notified when I publish!)

Don't miss out!

Visit the website below and you can sign up to receive emails whenever Shelley Tan publishes a new book. There's no charge and no obligation.

https://books2read.com/r/B-A-XYYT-FWBZB

BOOKS 2 READ

Connecting independent readers to independent writers.

Did you love *Better Late Than Forever*? Then you should read *Better Never Than Forever*[1] by Shelley Tan!

Valerie Parker and Kim Smith weren't exactly friends. Not that Kim had anything against Valerie for that matter, but Valerie was certainly not eager to begin a closeness with Kim after everything Kim had done to her best friend Char. Cheating on Char by screwing her husband? Despicable, Valerie had thought. But seeing as Valerie had moved past it (she was always so positive and mature about everything!) and the fact that there was no one else at Blue Ribbon to team up with for the Pas de Deux competition at the upcoming Dressage Championships in San Diego, Valerie decided to brush her personal feelings aside and spend time with Kim - strictly for enhancing her riding career, with a side-benefit of taking her mind off Duke, the low-life jerk of an ex-boyfriend who had recently broken her heart. It would take her mind off things, at least.

---

1. https://books2read.com/u/4NoanG

2. https://books2read.com/u/4NoanG

Kim had been reluctant to show her face at Blue Ribbon for quite some time after the entire debacle with Char's ex-husband, Jim. But at the urging of the dressage trainer, Petra, felt that perhaps it wouldn't hurt to begin riding again, as long as she kept a polite distance from Char. Kim had decided to swear off men for a while, and practicing on her horse Di Maggio was just the thing to get her mind off her troubles - not to mention her slight "transgressions"- while she focused on better days ahead. Preparing for the upcoming dressage competition would be just the thing to positively re-focus her energy.

Unsurprisingly, with so much in common between the horses and the recent break-ups with their boyfriends, Valerie found herself seeing Kim more as a friend who'd made a mistake than the adultress that she'd previously taken her for. I suppose that's why getting to know someone is so important, she surmised. It wasn't a surprise for Kim either, as she had vaguely known Valerie through Char and had seen her around the barn before the big "scandal," had occurred, and always thought she had seemed nice. What did come as a shock was when Kim began to realize that she could actually have feelings beyond friendship for her new Pas de Deux partner.

Which only caused more confusion when Duke unexpectedly showed up again, disrupting the budding friendship- and preparations- for the all-important show.

The resentment was beginning to build, and Kim wasn't sure she could handle it. Would Kim be able to get herself together and figure out her feelings before the big event? Or would she return to past habits and handle her feelings in a way that only caused more grief for everyone involved?

Find out in book 4 of the *Never Say Forever* series: **Better Never Than Forever**.

Read more at www.shelleytan.com.

Also by Shelley Tan

Never Say Forever
Better Late Than Forever
Better Never Than Forever

Watch for more at www.shelleytan.com.

About the Author

Shelley Tan is an educator and mother of twin boys. She grew up in Northern California but vacationed on Balboa Island in Southern California as a child with her family. Balboa Island was to her the happiest place on earth. Her debut novel, Better Late Than Forever, takes her and her reader back to that place where a romance she never expected occurs, and the chance to relive her childhood fairytale. When she is not working or writing, Shelley enjoys gardening and drinking wine, but not necessarily in that order.

Read more at www.shelleytan.com.

Ingram Content Group UK Ltd.
Milton Keynes UK
UKHW011945080523
421401UK00004B/345

9 798215 012741

Sofia Clark was newly divorced and looking to restart her life. Having spent summer on beautiful Balboa Island as a young girl and teenager, the magic that she felt as a child about Balboa Island had never left her, even after all these years. Now that her kids were grown and she found herself unexpectedly single, it dawned on her that she was free to move back to the place she had loved as a child, an opportunity that she never imagined she'd have. She quit her job as a principal in northern California and moved to Balboa Island to restart her life in the most magical and happiest place she had ever known. Once on the island, things went very smoothly for her until her heart led her to somewhere new, to a place she'd never even considered, until now.

Katrina Anderson was the superintendent, and Sofia's boss in her new position as the principal of Harbor Street Elementary. At 50 years old, Sofia had never been attracted to women. So what was it about Kat that suddenly drew Sofia to her? What were these unprecedented thoughts that she found herself pondering about Kat? Her children thought it was some sort of midlife crisis. Sofia wasn't sure. The only thing that she knew was that life was too short. Sofia felt compelled to risk everything in order to find out.

Shelley Tan is an educator and proud mother of twin boys. She grew up in Northern California but vacationed on Balboa Island in Southern California as a child with her family. Balboa Island was to her the happiest place on earth. Her debut novel, *Better Late Than Forever*, takes her and her reader back to that place where a romance she never expected occurs, and the chance to relive her childhood fairytale.

ISBN 979-8-215-01274-1

90000

9 798215 012741

Better Late Than Forever

Book 1 of the Never Say Forever Series

A Sapphic Romance by
Shelley Tan